CRÉ-WITCH CHRONICLES

CAST IN STONE

SARAH HEGGER

❀ Created with Vellum

DEDICATION

To Cynthia St-Aubin,
For so many reasons, but also for sharing with me
the beauty and wisdom of Druidry.

1

CRÉ-WITCH CHRONICLES

ngland, 1648

Maeve entered the wood and waited. Waterlogged ferns tangled around her bare ankles, dampening the hem of her gown. Dense fog roiled through the trees and wrapped her in ghostly tendrils.

Deep silence blanketed the grove as cold seeped into her bones.

"Sister." A wraith appeared between the slim, white trunks of the alder trees. "Blessed be."

Pressing her palms together, Maeve inclined her head to her guide. "Blessed be."

The guide's gown brightened from brown to blue and then flared silver as her presence strengthened in the sacred grove. "It is good you came."

As if Maeve had any choice in the matter. The dead summoned, and she came; that's what she did. "The passed are disturbed."

Dark shadows lurked beyond the alders, their coppery tang befouling the air.

"The spirits of the first stir. That's what troubles them."

The woman turned and watched the shadows. They darkened and red flashes of magic flickered in their depths. "The lost one creates a shift in power. The first sense her quickening."

"Is that why the grove is cold?" Maeve had never felt damp or cold in the grove before. She'd never seen the ever-present smudge of shadows loom as close either, and that smell...ugh!

Her guide nodded. "There is great peril ahead."

"What sort of peril?" Maeve paid more attention to her guide.

"She grows in power." The guide's form started to fade. "Ready yourself, Sister."

"Wait!" Maeve stepped toward the guide. "Ready myself for what?"

"Only one can bear the burden."

"What burden?" Maeve yelled, but the dead witch had already melted back into the trees.

Mist dipped and swirled and crept into the space the guide had occupied.

"Bloody hell!" Why did the dead always have to be so sodding cryptic? Instead of yammering on about power shifts and stirring ancients, they could save everyone a lot of time and tell her exactly what the problem was. When would be useful, as well. But, no, that wasn't their way.

A tree branch cracked and dropped soundlessly to the fern-choked floor. Where the branch had broken from the trunk, the alder's wood went from white to red. Sap oozed down the bark from the fresh wound.

Ask and you shall receive, apparently.

The alder's message was clear. Energies were out of balance and masculine energy was ascendant.

Beyond the alders, shadows swelled and flickered as if responding to the portent. Maeve shivered and dragged her gaze away. The embodiment of the lost one in the spirit realm, those shadows being so active meant more trouble than any living witch could handle.

Maeve released her hold on the spirit realm, and with a sucking whoosh, returned to her body momentarily disoriented. She blinked the present back into focus.

The present was exactly as she'd left it. The brazier from which she drew the power of her birth element, fire, was still burning, painting macabre shadows across sigils embedded in the cavern walls.

Here in the central cavern that guarded the Goddess Pool in its middle, sigils made of crystal, fossil and shell were the most prolific. The coppery tang of the spirit shadows lingered in her mouth and Maeve looked to the dark stain on the far side of the pool. There, the first had severed the lost one's connection with Goddess. The sigils bearing the lost one's story had died, meaning Maeve couldn't use them to walk into the witch's life they represented. In the lost one's case, not going near her was a good thing.

But she didn't need to walk beyond to know the story. A long time ago, the most powerful of the first four, Rhiannon, had gotten the idea that she deserved to be Goddess. It had almost killed the remaining three to repel her and cast her from the coven.

Drawing her cloak around her, Maeve left the central cavern via the arched doorway leading into the cavern beyond. Sigils gleamed enough light to illuminate her path as it twisted through another arched doorway into another cavern. The twists and turns through the web of caves beneath Baile Castle were as familiar to her as the shape of her face.

She reached the entrance cavern and sigils chimed a soft goodbye.

Outside the caverns, night had fallen. The moon hung high above the lazily undulating dark ocean.

The lingering gloom of her spirit walk stayed with her.

Given the lost one's involvement in her walk, she had to tell her coven leader but dealing with the dead was complicated. Everything was auguries and portents of doom with them, and she had to sift through the theatrics for the truth.

As disturbing as her latest walk had been, it hadn't given her anything certain. Something wicked was on its way, and it had to do with the lost one, who was getting stronger. All that added up to really, really bad news of the frustratingly vague sort.

Maeve didn't dislike the coven leader, but Fiona was friends with Edana, also Fiona's appointed second. A trip to Fiona inevitably meant a brush with Edana, and Maeve liked to hoard those for when she felt like taking a pot scourer to her pride.

The alder tree bothered her too. Ascendant male energy threatened war and violence. Not surprising, considering the way the Roundheads and Cavaliers were at each other throughout the country, but the alder's message had been specific. The cré-witches were headed for a tangle with male energy.

Edana's derision it was then. She left the caverns and climbed the cliff stairs. A stiff wind carried a hint of coming autumn, and it was a relief to step through the door at the top into the relative shelter of the walled bailey.

Dinner hour had come and gone during her spirit walk. As she opened the kitchen door, she was hit with a blast of savory, rich aromas, and her belly rumbled.

Cook entered from the pantries and stopped when she saw Maeve. Her smile of welcome was guarded. "Maeve."

"Cook." Maeve nodded. Any visit from her outside of normal business made her coven sisters nervous. "I missed dinner."

"Dinner?" Cook's reservation disappeared now that she knew Maeve wasn't here to collect anyone's spirit. "I have a nice ham joint left, and some cabbage if you fancy it."

The cabbage, not so much, but Maeve did like ham. Cook added an apple and some bread to a plate and brought them to Maeve.

She ate quickly and put away her plate before heading off to tackle Edana.

The great hall was nearly empty, except for a table of novices laughing and gossiping. One of them noticed Maeve and nudged her friend. All chatter stopped and they watched her cross the hall and take the grand staircase to the upper levels.

"Who do you think she's come for?" One of the novices whispered loud enough for Maeve to hear. "Do you think it's one of the older witches?"

She almost gave in to the temptation to turn about and head their way. Silly girls liked to whisper lurid tales and scare themselves about her. Maybe they should give her the scythe and cape and be done with it.

At the top of the stairs, she took a right down an empty passage toward Fiona's suite in the south tower. It was late, but Fiona was probably still awake. Maeve didn't fancy waking her up, but the threat of the lost one couldn't be ignored.

Light spilled from beneath Fiona's door.

Maeve tapped and entered.

Edana was wrapped around a man, her hands in his hair, her mouth glued to his.

His hands were filled with Edana's round bottom.

Face flaming, Maeve tried to back out, but the man raised his head and his gaze locked with hers.

Edana and Roderick? Maeve could hardly believe it. That was wrong, so wrong. Like a lion pairing up with a viper wrong. Roderick was a legend, the oldest and most powerful of the coimhdeacht, and Edana was...well...venomous. And also beautiful. As much as it galled Maeve to admit it, Edana was lovely and sensual. What man wouldn't notice?

"Maeve." Roderick tilted his head in greeting, not in the least embarrassed. His pale blue eyes almost dared her to say anything.

Still in his arms, Edana turned and scowled at her. "What do you want?"

"To see Fiona." Let the bloodletting begin.

"What for?" Edana scorched her with a look from top to toe and back again that disdained everything it touched. "It's too late for coven business." She turned back to Roderick. "Now go away."

If only she could. "I understand it's late, but this is important."

"Blast and hell, Maeve." Edana whirled back and stamped her foot. "Go away."

"I—"

"You're a bloody ghost hugger." Edana tossed her head. "What can a rabble of dead witches have to say that's so important it won't wait until morning?"

"That rabble of dead witches had plenty to say." Maeve held her ground. Edana had been taking swipes at her since girlhood. "And what they said can't wait until morning."

"Maeve?" Roderick disentangled himself and sidestepped Edana. "What did they tell you?"

Edana cuddled up to his arm and pressed her breasts against him. "Ignore her. She's like a cockroach. Eventually she scuttles back to her dark hole."

The insult was bad enough, but Roderick's look of pity made her wish for a dark hole to crawl into.

"Maeve?" Roderick studied her.

Roderick intimidated her. Edana was just a bitch, but one she was used to. "I wouldn't bother you, but Fiona needs to know this."

"You're right about the first part. You shouldn't bother me." Edana motioned the door. She wrapped her arms around

Roderick's neck and smiled a slow, sensual invitation up at him. "I have much better things to do."

Maeve would give both arms not to be standing there watching them.

Roderick shifted away from her and walked up to Maeve, sucking all the air out of the room as he drew closer. All young witches developed crushes on Roderick. He was so large, and handsome, and the tragic tale of his lost love was the stuff girlish fantasies were made of. It was a good thing they all grew out of those crushes. Maeve forced herself not to fidget, but there was nothing she could do about the slow spread of heat up her neck to her face.

"The passed told you something." Roderick stopped two feet in front of her. He had this way of looking at someone as if they were the only being in existence. It felt a bit like standing directly in the sun. "And it disturbed you enough to bring you here."

"It's nothing definite." Her mind emptied of thought and her body of air. "It's bad. Very bad. And also some words. And the shadows. Also, the alder. The alder was the most specific."

A gentle smile tilted Roderick's mouth up. "Tell me about the alder. And this very bad thing." A hint of laughter creased the corners of his eyes.

Maeve needed to pull herself together and get coherent. "The—"

"Roderick," Edana whined. "Why are you bothering with her? She's nothing."

The laughter disappeared from his eyes and he frowned at Edana over his shoulder. "She's the spirit walker, and there is only ever one in the coven at any time. You should accord her more respect."

Edana gaped and then threw Maeve a murderous look, as if she was somehow responsible for Roderick's rebuke.

Maeve smirked and wished she could claim the credit.

"You're coven sisters." Roderick extended the minatory look to her now. "And you need to be an example to the novices who are learning from you."

That was the other thing about Roderick. He was bossy and commanding, which helped shake Maeve out of her moment of girlish admiration. "I was called by the spirits earlier this evening." The sooner she delivered her message, the sooner she could leave. "My guide had a warning that the first are stirring and there's great danger threatening us."

Edana huffed. "Is that it? You barged in here about some vague warning." She stared down her nose at Maeve. "And don't you think if there was something to worry about the seers would have been up here before you?"

Edana was right, she really was, and Maeve hadn't thought of the seers. If the lost one was moving, and coming as strongly as the spirit realm suggested, then surely the seers would have gathered portents. Still, she would bite her tongue before she admitted as much to Edana. "I'm not a seer. I can only tell you what I see in the spirit realm. Tonight, my guide told me the first were concerned about the lost one quickening. I saw for myself how she grows in strength beyond."

"What does that mean to you?" Roderick kept his gaze on her, and Maeve empathized with how a doe must feel when a wolf had her on his menu.

"If she grows in strength beyond, then it could mean she grows in strength here." Maeve spoke to Roderick. If she left her message with Edana, it would never get to Fiona. Roderick, however, could and would decide if it had to go to Fiona. "Beyond mirrors this realm."

Roderick cocked his head. "Tell me about the alder?"

"A branch broke off and the wound bled."

Roderick had been around since the first. He would understand tree lore.

"Gosh!" Edana rolled her eyes. "I'll never sleep again."

If Edana knew anything about trees and their messages, she really wouldn't sleep, but then Edana's nighttime activities, according to coven gossip, didn't leave much time for learning and speculation.

"The alder speaks to strength and battle. It's a protector. Baile feels something too. The castle is...uneasy," Roderick said, his gaze growing unfocused for a moment before snapping back to her. "You did right to bring this to me. I'll make sure to speak to Fiona about this."

As head of the coimdeacht, Roderick had the security of the castle and the protection of all witches as his primary duty. If she could trust anyone with the portent, it would be him.

"I have to report anything linked to the lost one," she said.

"Understandably. No sane person would choose to tangle with that bitch if they could avoid it." Roderick had been there the day the first had severed her from Goddess; he would know. "Can you spirit walk again? Perhaps find out more."

"I could." Maeve got her hand on the door latch. "I'll use a more reliable guide next time. One who speaks more plainly."

"You're such a ghoul." Edana gave an exaggerated shudder. "Never mind alder branches breaking. You're the creepiest thing in here tonight."

And that was enough for one night. Maeve opened the door and left.

2

C hatter rose and fell as ninety cré-witches sat down to dinner. Ninety women did a lot of talking, and when they were angry, they did a lot of seething. And there was a lot more talking than eating going on in the hall tonight. Most of it was about the witch-hunts and the decree from Fiona that had followed it: no more unsanctioned trips outside Baile.

Maeve could spread the atmosphere on her bread, it was so thick.

Arguments for and against the decree raged all around her.

"Our purpose is amongst Goddess's creation." Lavina jabbed her finger at Colleen across the table. "We can't ignore people to save our hides."

Maeve dipped her flaky, buttery pastry into rich, meaty gravy and ate it. If only they hadn't put kidneys in the pie, she could enjoy it so much more.

Colleen sighed. "But we can't ignore the threat to us either."

"We have protection." Lavina jerked her head to her and Colleen's coimhdeacht, the warriors bonded to them.

Colleen sighed. "But that's only those of us who are bonded." She leaned closer to Lavina and whispered, "And soon we'll add a new sister to our number."

"Blessed." Sitting to Lavina's right, Thomas shook his head at Colleen, but a half smile softened the admonishment. "That's coimhdeacht business and not to be discussed here."

"Oh, all right." Colleen wrinkled her nose at him.

Lavina laughed and nudged Thomas. "You're far too pretty to be such a fussy old maid."

Thomas shook his head and chuckled.

Maeve agreed with Lavina. Thomas was very easy on the eye. So easy that she liked sneaking glances at him. Sometimes he even glanced back with a wink or a smile.

"What do you think?" Lavina turned to her.

Maeve stopped chewing her pastry. Witches tended to cluster by blessing. As the only spirit walker, and also spending the amount of time she did with the dead, she was not often drawn into dinner conversation. She swallowed quickly. "We're cré-witches. We were created to bring her creation into closer communion with Goddess. We can't do that locked up in a castle."

"Well said, Maeve." Thomas smiled at her.

Her cheeks heated. She'd wager she looked as awkward as she felt, but then the dead didn't demand social skills.

When only kidney pieces remained, she took her plate to the serving hatch and called her thanks to Cook and her helpers.

Out in the bailey a low moon rode a cloud-laden sky. Opening the sea door, she alighted the cliff stairs. Sharp briny sea tang blew fresh in her face.

In the caverns, mellifluous chimes of thousands of crystals greeted her. As she walked through the caverns, crystals, shells and fossils that formed the patterns glowed as the souls of departed witches responded to her caress on their sigils.

"Sister."

"Walk with us."

"We must speak with you."

Spoken as ghostly whispers in her mind, the voices of the dead only she could hear. Like the rest of the coven, even the dead were unsettled and she toyed with taking the spirit walk she'd promised Roderick.

Tonight, though, was her favorite night of the month. She aimed to enjoy her monthly appointment in the village.

Once she reached the central cavern, Maeve slipped on her long cloak and raised the hood. Love her visits as she did, with everything happening in the village, she wasn't about to announce herself to anybody who happened to be hanging about.

Maeve hurried to the far corner where a rock outcrop hid her from sight. Putting her hand against the rock, she muttered the incantation she had learned from witches now beyond.

The sigils chimed a soft warning to her. Even they looked askance at how she used the passage. They were patterns embedded into cavern walls, however, and not a living breathing woman who wanted to share her blessing. "Sorry," she whispered.

The rock slid open soundlessly and Maeve hurried into the damp, dark maw. She snapped her fingers and fire answered her call in a flare of red tendrils that coalesced into a small flame that danced in the air and lit her way. It was later than normal, and the rest of the village would be tucked up against the night.

The passage ran from the caverns and far beneath the castle as it wound toward the village. It ended in more rock and she muttered the incantation again. The rock opened and she released fire. It flared and disappeared, leaving the scent of orange and lilies behind.

Maeve stepped into the crypt below the village church. At the western end of the crypt, she found the small hidden door leading into the churchyard and opened it. The stairs to the churchyard above were slick with moss and damp, and she trod carefully.

Popping her head over the edge, she first ascertained the churchyard abandoned before she left the safety of the stairwell.

A few lost souls flitted about their grave markers, unable or unwilling to go beyond. Frightened she could force them beyond against their will, lingering spirits veered away from her. It didn't work like that, but there was no reasoning with the lingerers. They were trapped in the moment of their death in an endless loop. Eventually it drove them mad.

The road in front of the churchyard was deserted, and Maeve hurried along it toward the beckoning rectangles of light marking the village houses. Excitement thrummed through her veins. Even had someone been about, in the dark she could pass for a young village woman on her way home.

The latch on the gate clicked as she opened it. They had oiled the hinges since her last visit. The cottage curtains were drawn, but through a slight chink, warm, yellow light peeked.

With a quick glance about, Maeve tapped on the door.

A stout matron peered through the chink.

"Good evening, Rebecca." Maeve kept her voice low.

Rebecca opened the door wide and motioned Maeve inside.

Leaning out the door, Rebecca checked the night for prying eyes. She closed and latched the door behind them. "With all the troubles, we were worried you might not come."

"I'm careful." Maeve nodded to the other occupants of the cottage and took her place amongst them at the table. Three she knew. The fourth woman would be the one who needed her blessing.

A long, fat candle flickered in the center of the table. All of the women had a bag of mending and some needles and thread in front of them. If anyone happened upon them, they were a sewing circle.

Bustling over, Rebecca took her seat at Maeve's right. "Ladies." She nodded to each of the four women staring at Maeve. She held her hands out to Maeve and the woman beside her. "Before we begin, I would remind all to keep this meeting a secret." She lowered her voice. "On pain of death."

The younger, blond woman across from Maeve rolled her eyes. "Everybody knows not to shout this about. Can we get on with it? Fred is waiting for his dinner."

"You don't have to be here, Jane." Rebecca sniffed. "It's not like the blessed needs you."

Jane leaned forward and glared. "I'm part of this, and don't you forget it."

"Let's begin." Maeve smiled. Rebecca and Jane could argue for hours. She looked at the visitor. "I'm Maeve."

The woman paled and stared at her with wide eyes. "Pru." She swallowed and cleared her throat. "Prudence. My name is Prudence."

"I'm pleased to meet you." Maeve tried to look reassuring, but people were always nervous their first time. "Would you like to tell me why you're here?"

Prudence glanced at the other women.

Plump and sweet faced, Molly gave Prudence a nod of encouragement. "Go ahead and ask her. Maeve can really talk to the dead. You'll be amazed."

"Right." Prudence clasped her fingers together so tightly, her knuckles whitened. "That's why I'm here. I need to..." She faltered and looked at Molly. "Are you sure this isn't a mortal sin?"

Maeve sat back and let the village women deal with their guest.

"Now, Pru." Molly patted Prudence's clenched hands. "We've been over this. You need to ask your mother about the locket." She beamed a reassuring smile at Prudence. "Your mother is in heaven, isn't she? How can that be a sin?"

"Fred makes my life a misery if he has to wait for his dinner." Jane sighed and rolled her eyes. "If you don't want to do this, fine. We can all go home, and Maeve can get back to the castle."

"No!" Prudence straightened and gulped. "I need to find that locket. It's mine and I want it."

The rapacious gleam in Prudence's eye gave Maeve a sinking feeling. It wasn't going to go well. What mattered to the living held no weight with the departed.

"All right then." Rebecca held her hands out again. "Let's begin."

The handholding wasn't necessary, but Maeve let the villagers have their rituals. She drew fire from the candle and slid into the outer edges of beyond. The scent of her working blessing filled the cottage.

"I can smell oranges," Prudence said. "And...lilies. Why is that?"

"It's her magic, dear." Molly took a deep sniff. "I think it smells lovely."

Pru's sharp whisper sounded like it came from down a long tunnel. "Why are her eyes all milky like that?"

"Hush!" Jane said. "Let the blessed work."

The edge of beyond opened as a warm, sunbathed meadow. Blue and pink wildflowers swayed gently in the balmy breeze. A pretty brunette stood in the middle of the meadow. The passed chose their appearance and Prudence's mother had taken the form of her younger self. "Who are you?"

"I'm Maeve." Maeve stood still and let the girl study her.

"I'm Beth," she said. "Why are you shining?"

She often got this. "Because I'm still of the living. You're seeing my life force shining through me."

"Oh." Beth's pretty face creased into a frown and she looked down at her hands. "I'm not shining. Does that mean I'm dead?"

"You have passed." Maeve nodded. "You'll remain here until you're ready to return."

Beth looked up at her. "Oh, I like that. When will that be?"

"Only you know that." From the cottage, Pru was demanding to know how much longer this would take. Maeve needed to hurry things along. "Your daughter, Prudence, has sent me to ask you something."

Beth's girlish form thickened into that of her later years. Gray streaked her hair and lines creased her face. "Is she well? Bert isn't a good husband." She chewed the edge of her thumb-nail. "I told her not to marry him, but would she listen?"

"She needs to know about a locket." Maeve brought Beth back on topic. The passed could ramble on endlessly. They had infinite time to chatter.

Beth frowned and gave Maeve a sharp glare. "Why does she want to know about that?"

Splitting herself between the two realms took more power from her gift and Maeve drew deeper on fire. The candle flared. The women at the table jerked back.

Prudence squeaked and glanced about her. "Is this usual?"

"Your mother is with me," Maeve's voice sounded strange to her own ears. "She wants to know why you want the locket."

"Really?" Prudence leaned forward, her cheeks flushing. "How do I know she's really there?"

Jane snorted. "You doubt the blessed?"

"Anyone could say they were with my mother," Prudence said. "Just last week Martha from up Oak Lane said she saw the Virgin Mary in her milking pail. I saw that smear and it didn't look anything like the Blessed Virgin."

Maeve looked at Beth. "She needs proof that it's you. Tell me something only you would know."

"I don't care to." Beth jammed her hands on her hips. "You

tell Prudence if she and Hope are fighting about that locket, I won't tell either of them where it is. They both know I want it to go to my sister-in-law."

Maeve repeated Beth's words.

Prudence stared at her. "But she's not even blood."

"I'm done with this." Beth appeared as her younger self again and turned and flounced off. The meadow vanished and Maeve returned to Rebecca's kitchen. "She's gone."

"What? Why?" Prudence gripped the table edge. "She didn't tell me where the locket is."

"I'm sorry." Maeve shrugged. "I have no control over what she tells me."

"This is nonsense." Prudence frowned and pushed away from the table, her chair shrieking against the floor. "You're a deceiver."

Molly put out a placating hand. "Prud—"

"I knew this couldn't be real." Prudence looked at Maeve with raw loathing. "Nobody can commune with the dead. It's evil." Her gaze grew narrow and angry. "You hags will get what is coming to you. See if you don't."

3

The cottage rocked from the force with which Prudence slammed the door.

"Who chose her?" Jane glared at Rebecca and Molly. "I could have told you she wasn't the right sort."

Molly wrinkled her nose. "But she seemed so upset about the locket. I thought she wanted it for comfort after the loss of her mother."

Jane snorted and folded her arms. "If she goes to Father Steven with her story, we're all in for it."

"She won't do that." Rebecca didn't look nearly as certain as she sounded. "Will she?"

"I've heard talk about the witch-hunts." Around the coven it was mainly speculation. They could be what her spirit walk had been referring to.

Jane shook her head. "It's not just talk. Not two days ago the midwife from Abbotsham was drowned."

"Drowned?"

Rebecca grimaced. "Trial by water, and that horrible Mathew Hopkins is strutting about calling himself Witchfinder General."

"What's a trial by water?" That sounded like Fiona was right to worry about the safety of the witches outside Baile Castle. Not that Maeve agreed with isolating themselves, but more caution sounded like a jolly good idea.

"They tie you up and toss you in a river," Molly answered with morbid delight. "If you drown, it means you're innocent, but if you don't, then they say the water wouldn't have you and it must mean you're guilty. Then they kill you."

Jane glared at her. "That's ridiculous. Either way you're dead."

"And what if you know how to swim?" Rebecca sucked in her cheeks. "My dad taught me how to swim when I was little."

"They did this to the midwife?" Maeve didn't want to stop her visits to the village, but she wasn't like the healers who came to help with sickness, or the wardens who could coax good crops from the earth, or the guardians who had the affinity for animals. Her visits were for herself, but they couldn't continue if they put those three women in danger.

"Yes." Molly shuddered and her eyes gleamed. "They say she didn't last four minutes and now Abbotsham is looking for a new midwife."

Greater Littleton couldn't afford to lose their midwife. Jane would need her services any day now.

Maeve stood and gathered her cloak. It made her want to weep to say, "I think it best if we take a small break from sewing circle."

"Oh, no." Molly's voice quavered. "I do so love your visits."

So did Maeve. They made her feel useful to the living. "I'm sorry, but the sewing circle could be putting us all in danger."

"She's right." Jane stood and twitched the skirts of her gown around her swollen, pregnant belly. "Once this has all died down, we can start the sewing circle again."

Foreboding slid down Maeve's spine. She didn't think she would attend sewing circle again. She looked at sweet Molly, acerbic Jane and ever-practical Rebecca, impressing their faces into her memories. She couldn't say she knew them well, but they were her connection with life outside the castle, and she enjoyed her time with them.

"Nothing to worry about, dear." Rebecca patted her shoulder. "This Cromwell rebellion has everyone stirred up. You cré-witches are wonderful women." She squeezed Maeve's shoulder. "Everyone in the village knows it. You take such good care of us."

Jane snorted. "You overestimate the good sense of most folk."

"Everything will be fine." Rebecca glared at Jane and folded her arms. "You'll see."

"I'm sure you're right." Molly frowned and glanced from Rebecca to Jane. She gave Maeve a tremulous smile. "But maybe you're right about giving this a rest. Just until everything quiets down again."

"I think having a break is for the best." Maeve gave all three women a quick hug. "Take care of yourselves."

Slipping into the night, she hurried through the dark to the churchyard. Her spirit walk had her imagining trouble where there was none. There was no reason sewing circle couldn't start again when all this unpleasantness had blown over. It had been more than unpleasantness for the poor woman in Abbotsham.

The breeze kicked up and scattered leaves across the road. Maeve shivered and huddled deeper into her cloak. The night felt wrong somehow, ominous.

A dog barked and startled her, and she kept to the far side of the road.

"What is up with that bloody dog?" A door opened, spilling light across the road. A man stood silhouetted in the entrance. "Come 'ere you daft bugger."

Wagging its tail, the dog darted into the house and the man shut the door again.

Maeve waited a few breaths before hurrying on. Perhaps now that her visits to the village were paused, she should ask the guardians for a dog to keep her company. There were always plenty of animals about the castle.

A woman's laugh, husky and full of promise came from a small home to her right.

No curtains obstructed her view, and a lantern bathed the cottage in golden light.

Maeve's hackles rose and her stomach lurched.

"Sister! Take heed." The soft whisper carried the cold echo of beyond. Whatever was happening in that cottage was linked to the warning she'd received. She crept closer.

The fire in the cottage hearth called to her and she greeted it.

Inside, the cottage looked like almost every other in the village. A cradle rested close to the hearth's warmth. Beside a rough table in the center of the room, a pretty woman stood before a man and laughed up at him. Her eyes gleamed an invitation as she bit her bottom lip. "I'm glad you came."

"Are you now, Agnes?" Maeve couldn't be completely sure, but the man didn't sound like he came from the village. His deep, smooth voice sounded a lot more like a noble than a villager. He had his back to Maeve, but he was tall and broad shouldered, and his jacket looked to be velvet.

Maeve's flesh crawled, but she couldn't draw away from the cottage.

Hand on her hip, Agnes thrust her bosom toward the man. She breathed deep, causing her flesh to swell over her bodice. Her smile was pure invitation. "You know you're always welcome here."

"How gratifying." The man stroked the slope of Agnes's breast with the back of his fingers.

Maeve's gaze locked on the man. Shadows, dark and thick and cloying, swirled in the air around him. The dark crawled across her skin and she rubbed her arms to dispel the sensation. She wanted to run away, but her legs refused to move.

"Alexander," Agnes whispered, more breath than word, and closed her eyes. She dropped her head back, her face awash with sensual delight as he curved his long fingers around her breast. "Touch me. Please."

Maeve opened her mouth to scream at Agnes to run, not to let him touch her, but no sound came out.

"Who do you belong to, Agnes?" Alexander swept his thumb over Agnes's nipple.

Prickles rasped over Maeve's skin, sharp and uncomfortable. A cold, metallic tang filled her mouth and nostrils, and her stomach lurched. It was the same scent as the lost one's shadows. The man was connected to her.

Agnes moaned. "You. Only you."

"Then—" Alexander's spine snapped straight, and his hand stilled. He turned his head to the side. A predatory smile tilted his full mouth. "Hello, my pretty mouse. Aren't you a lovely surprise?"

Maeve lurched into the dark beyond the window. Her heart pounded and sweat broke over her.

Agnes blinked as if waking from a dream. "Who are you speaking to? Who is there?"

Turning fully, Alexander's gaze locked on where Maeve stood shivering in the dark. He took a deep breath and his smile grew sensual. "You smell delicious, little mouse. Do you want to play?"

Maeve whirled about and forced her shaking legs to run.

Behind her, the cottage door opened, and Alexander's laughter chased her into the night. A midnight black tendril rode the breeze, chasing her. His smooth, rich voice sounded right beside her ear. "Run along, little cré-witch. We'll meet again soon."

Maeve's heart didn't stop pounding even when she reached the safety of Baile once more. As if Alexander was chasing her, Maeve ran through the caverns, up the stairs and across the bailey.

When she entered the castle, she slowed to a quick walk. The uneasy sensation stayed with her as she hurried up the stairs toward her chamber. Her blood thrummed in her ears and her hands shook.

A shape appeared in the corridor in front of her. Maeve leaped back. Her foot tangled in her skirts and she lost her balance.

Big hands caught her and righted her. "Steady on."

Heart pounding, Maeve yanked at the grip on her arms.

"Maeve." The grip tightened. A strong presence steadied her. "Stop. Breathe!"

The voice penetrated her fright and she stopped fighting. Fear drained away and she sagged. "It's you."

"It's me." Roderick drew her against him. His heartbeat beneath her ear. "And you're safe."

She was, and every part of her knew it. Maeve peered up and up some more into his pale blue eyes. Her head spun and she had to force the next breath into her lungs. "Sorry." Her voice came out breathy and girly. "I didn't see you there."

"Clearly." Roderick frowned down at her, his chiseled features wearing the expression well. "What had you running as if your life was at risk?"

She couldn't tell him. Not tell anyone really, but especially not him in case it got back to Edana. Maeve would wager her life Edana wouldn't hesitate to tell Fiona.

"Nothing." Maeve cursed the way her voice squeaked out of her. She had to do better. "I saw a rat."

"A rat?" Up went one eyebrow. "You, a spirit walker, are afraid of a little rat?"

Not trusting her voice, she nodded.

Roderick stared at her.

She locked her knees and restrained the desire to fidget. "It was a big rat."

"I see. A big rat," he said, still giving her that searching stare that made her think he could see right through her clothing. "You're out late. Shouldn't you be abed already?"

"Shouldn't you?" She gave Edana's door a pointed stare.

Roderick raised a sculpted dark brow. "At least I have a good reason for being here in the middle of the night."

Maeve would hardly call it a good reason. "As do I." Nothing attached to Edana was ever good in her book, but that wasn't a discussion she planned to have with Roderick. "I was in the caverns until late, and now I'm tired. Which is probably why the rat frightened me. I'm tired and not thinking straight." She managed to force a yawn and stepped back from him. "See there. Tired, so tired."

Folding his arms, he watched her.

Maeve edged another step back.

At last, Roderick broke the silence. "Did you take that spirit walk yet? The one with the guide you know better."

"Not yet. But I will tomorrow." Time to make her escape. "Which means, I'd better get my rest."

"You do that."

Maeve dared not look at him as she said, "Well, I'm off for bed."

"Alone?"

His question stopped her in her tracks and snapped her gaze up to his. "Yes."

Roderick smirked. "What a pity." He sauntered past her and through Edana's door. "Good night, Maeve. Sleep well. Alone."

4

Maeve's encounter with the strange and disturbing Alexander kept her up well into the small hours. He had something to do with the lost one. He stank of her, and the tendril that had chased her exuded the same ominous sensation she associated with the spirit realm shadows.

Dawn was only an hour or so away when she gave up on sleep, dressed and went to the caverns instead.

As she crossed the threshold into the caverns, thousands of sigils chimed a greeting. Slowly, she walked from cavern to cavern, letting the familiarity and welcome of the passed calm and center her.

In the central cavern, she prepared for her spirit walk. Pulling out her anchoring crystal of carnelian, Maeve whispered her prayer for protection, "Goddess, beneficent and benign, walk with me now amongst all blessed who came before, all blessed who now are, and all blessed yet to come."

She snapped her fingers and two braziers flared to life. The childlike joy of being able to do that never diminished. Flame strained toward her, and she held out her palm for it. Playfully the flame danced across her palms.

Maeve tethered a power line to her anchoring crystal and then drew on her birth element to awaken her blessing. The twining aromas of lilies and oranges filled her nose and coated her tongue. What she did in the village was child's play and involved only a portion of her blessing. A bit like dipping a toe into the lake's edge.

Now she sought to swim in the lake, and she pulled more strength from fire. Braziers flared four feet high as fire responded to her request.

Maeve laid her palms on the sigils.

Her gift led her into a familiar pretty glade beside a deep blue pool. Shadows darkened the sky above a willow draping its fronds on the ground. Again with those shadows so very present. Maeve parted the fronds and stepped into the green bower created by the tree.

As Maeve had known she would, a witch stood with her hand against the willow's trunk. Not much older than Maeve, she had the same flaxen hair and blue eyes.

"Moira." Maeve greeted her great, great grandmother. "I have need of you."

"Ah, Maeve. I'm glad you came." Moira's blue eyes filled with tears.

Moira had never wept before, and Maeve's sense of uneasiness grew closer to fear. "Do you know what's wrong? Have you heard why the first stir?"

"They are frightened, Maeve. We all are." She shuddered. "We feel the shadows grow and grow. We see true death ahead. Many witches will pass beyond, but even worse will be the witches who don't."

Maeve had come to Moira not only because they shared blood, but because Moira was more blunt than many of the other guides. "Are you saying a lot of witches will die?"

"Aye." Moira's answer chilled Maeve to the bone. "And worse."

"How do we prevent it?" Maybe they were telling her because it wasn't too late to prevent disaster. "Tell me what to do, and I'll see it done."

"Aye, you will." Moira met her gaze, and in the blue depths of her eyes, Maeve read so much grief it reached within her and nestled in her chest like an open wound. "You're the one," Moira said. "You will bear the burden."

"What burden?" That didn't make any sense. Moira couldn't go all mysterious on her now. "If my coven sisters are in danger, you need to help me conquer whatever this danger is."

Moira shook her head. Red tears slid down her cheeks. "I can't."

"You can." Maeve stepped closer. She refused to let Moira poof away without telling her more. "Just tell me and I'll do it. Tell me."

Already waning, Moira shook her head again. "The burden must be carried, but you won't carry it alone."

Maeve screamed her frustration as Moira disappeared. In the caverns, she moved her hands along the wall. Her vision lurched and she was sitting beside a lily-laden pond. The shadows followed her. An older witch looked up and started when she saw Maeve. "The one who bears the burden."

Maeve gentled her tone. "What burden?"

The witch faded into nothing.

Maeve sought another sigil and her spirit shifted to a sandy beach. Waves crashed on the shore beneath the looming shadows. Two witches stood by the water's edge holding hands as they watched the shadows roil above them.

"We weep for you, little sister." One looked at her. Red tears streaked her cheeks. "The burden you must bear will be weighty."

The other one looked at her too. "But you won't bear it alone."

They faded, and the wind blew them away.

Again Maeve moved to another sigil, and found another soul. And again, and again and again, but the result was always the same. The witches were weeping tears of blood and telling her about some bedamned burden she must bear. And those cursed shadows. Everywhere she went, they were there.

It was well past noon when she returned to her body in the cavern. She'd been gone a long time and her flesh was cold. However, the chill to her physical form was nothing compared to the deeper chill inside her.

Whatever was coming was bad, awful, and there didn't seem to be any way to avoid it.

This warranted another trip to Fiona.

She hurried from the caverns and into the castle. Maeve wished she had specific information for Fiona. Logic suggested the danger was connected to the witch-hunts. How the lost one was involved, she had no idea. Moira had said many witches would die, and worse. True death was the only thing worse than physical death, and even thinking about it made her shiver. To be forever separated from Goddess, trapped in the present with no chance of returning and continuing your soul's journey was so much worse than physical death.

Surely they weren't in danger as long as they stayed inside Baile. Now she was sounding more and more like she supported Fiona's decree about leaving the castle.

Halfway across the bailey, she nodded a greeting to a stout woman with a serious face. "Good day, Sheila."

"Spirit Walker." Sheila hurried on. They'd been good friends before Siobhan had passed and Maeve had inherited the blessing of spirit walker. At the time of her selection, Maeve and Sheila had been training as healers together. Now Sheila was a full healer and insisted on calling her by her blessing and not her name. Not so long ago, she and Sheila had huddled together and whispered secrets to each other.

Being the only spirit walker could be lonely at times.

After she spoke to Fiona, she might find Roderick and tell him what she had discovered. He hadn't dismissed her as ridiculous the other night.

Before interrupting his tryst with Edana, Maeve couldn't recall her last encounter with Roderick. As first coimhdeacht, Roderick was always about the keep doing manly things with weapons and combat.

Three apprentices ran down the corridor, giggling and whispering to each other. They were so intent on their conversation they went right past her without one of them remembering to shudder.

They reminded her of how she and Sheila used to be. Like most girls who had grown up in the castle, they had also gone through their period of sighing and casting languid gazes at Roderick. It was something of a right of passage for novice cré-witches.

For his part, Roderick never took any notice of the young girls. Until they got older. Like Edana.

Maeve ran up the stairs to Fiona's chambers.

A second group of girls, novices this time, brushed passed her on the stairs, nearly knocking her over in their enthusiasm.

This time Maeve rapped and waited before opening Fiona's door.

Edana looked up from where she sat by the fire. Tall and graceful with rounded hips and a full bosom above her flat belly, it was hard to find a physical flaw in Edana. No wonder Roderick kept her company at night. She looked down her perfect nose at Maeve. "What?"

"I need to see Fiona." Maeve slid around the door into the room. Edana always made her feel less in every way. "It's important."

"That's what you said the other night." Edana sneered as she stood. "Roderick will deal with it when he can. Now, run along."

"I can't." This was too important to let her and Edana's mutual dislike get in the way. "I've had more warnings and they're serious."

"You're overreacting." Edana caressed the bodice of her beautiful gold silk gown. "Again."

"I really am not." Maeve didn't own a gown near as lovely as that. She kept her temper in check. "It can't wait."

"It will have to." Edana tossed her head. "Because she's not here."

"Where is she? I'll find her," Maeve said. It struck her that Edana wasn't looking as venomous as she usually did. Edana had an expectant excited glow about her, like she was hugging a delicious secret. "If you'll tell me where she is."

Edana sauntered over to the mirror above the mantle and examined her reflection. She patted a hair back into place and pinched her cheeks.

"Edana." Holding on to her patience, Maeve tried to imbue her voice with the seriousness of her task. "I need to see her."

"You can't." Edana raised her chin and preened at her reflection. "Because she's with the coimhdeacht."

Fiona wasn't bonded. Could Roderick have told her what Maeve had said? "Why?"

"Not that it's anything to do with you, but even you'll find out anyway." Edana's broad smile grew insufferably smug. "The coimhdeacht are calling a bonding."

Edana's news shook Maeve out of her purpose for a moment. "A bonding? They haven't called a bonding for..." She couldn't remember how long, certainly not in her lifetime.

"They're calling one now." Edana leaned closer to the mirror and scrutinized her reflection. With a satisfied smirk, she straightened. "Goddess has called him back to service and Roderick is to bond a new witch."

As Maeve stood there and gaped at her, Edana sailed past. She stopped when she drew abreast and whispered in Maeve's ear. "The ceremony is due to start any minute. If you hurry you'll get a good view of Roderick bonding me."

Seriousness of her message aside, a bonding was big news. Huge. Even if it was Edana being bonded, and Maeve was very much afraid Edana was right about that. Roderick had only ever bonded two witches in his time as coimhdeacht. The most notable of which was Tahra, one of the first, and according to coven rumor, the love of his life.

The bonding had lasted for two hundred years until Tahra, already ancient even back then, had chosen to go beyond. Tahra had taken Roderick's heart with her, and forever made him the tragic hero of novice fantasies.

If Edana was telling the truth, she would have to wait. And if Edana was telling the truth, Maeve really didn't want to miss it.

Maeve hurried to the hall and joined the stream of sisters heading for the barracks. Even as the great bell chimed for them to gather, the witches were already ahead of its announcement. Keeping anything secret amongst ninety women was impossible.

Their chatter filled the passageway that led to the main arena. A large, oval room with a sandy floor, it was normally where the coimhdeacht sparred and practiced. Tonight all other light had been extinguished.

In darkness, the witches gathered at the edges of the arena.

Around Maeve her coven sisters speculated.

"It's because of the witch-hunts," a shorter sister to Maeve's left said. "That's why Goddess has called him back into bondage." She leaned closer to her friend. "I heard they're having a trial in the village as we stand here."

Her friend didn't look impressed with the news. She looked about her and sighed. "I've heard the same thing every day just about. I don't listen to gossip."

Maeve suppressed a snort. She'd be the only witch who didn't listen to gossip. She caught the witch who had spoken first by the sleeve. "What trial in the village?"

"I don't know, but I wouldn't pay it much mind. As Rowena says, we hear about witch trials and whatnot every day," she said.

Rowena nodded. "Our villagers love us. They've no reason to fear witchcraft." Then she leaned closer to her friend. "Who do you think he'll bond?"

"I bet it's Edana."

"Everyone thinks it's Edana," Rowena whispered back. "She's a warden, and they say she's as strong as Fiona."

"She is." The shorter one gave an emphatic nod. "I've seen her make rock melt."

"No." Rowena gave her a look loaded with doubt. "That's not possible."

Maeve shared her skepticism. Edana wasn't all that strong.

"It is, too." Shorty bristled. "I saw it with my own eyes. And anyway, it makes sense for him to bond a warden. They go out of the castle more than the others."

"I wish I was a warden." Rowena sighed.

Shorty giggled. "Only because you want Roderick to bond you."

Maeve suppressed a grin. Nothing much changed from generation to generation.

"Or Thomas." Rowena giggled.

"But he's Lavina's."

"It's not like she owns him." Rowena glared at Shorty.

Shorty huffed. "She may as well. They've been bonded for over eighty years."

The coimhdeacht had been formed to protect a witch when

she left the safety of Baile. Even if her life was threatened, no cré-witch could ever use her powers to hurt another living creature. The coimhdeacht were under no such vow.

"Doesn't she look lovely?" A witch in front of Maeve pointed at Edana, standing beside Fiona at the opposite end of the arena. She'd added a long, gauzy veil to her hair, and looked like a faerie princess. If anybody had asked her, Maeve would've said she thought the look a bit overwrought.

Fiona looked as smug as Edana. They had been friends since childhood, both of them warden witches too.

Light flickered in the passage leading deeper into the coimhdeacht's part of the castle.

Silence swept over the witches.

First came the bonded witches dressed in flowing white robes, their hair unbound, they each carried a large white candle. They moved to the outer edge of the arena and stood facing the gathered audience.

Nearest to Maeve, Lavina stood, her candle painting sinister shadows across her normally pleasant face. She didn't look a day over five and twenty, but Maeve knew she was much, much older than that.

Silently the coimhdeacht entered behind them. Wearing long robes belted at the waist, they each carried a silver sword. Candlelight caught on their wickedly sharp blades and threw reflections over their hard, grave faces. Standing back to back with their bonded witches, the coimhdeacht faced the inside of the arena.

Thomas spoke from in front of Lavina, so suddenly that Maeve jumped. "Brother! You are called."

Roderick entered the arena and stood in the center.

The quality of the silence in the arena deepened.

The coimhdeacht spoke together. "Brother, you are called."

"I hear the call." Roderick's voice, strong and sure, carried around the arena.

"Brother, do you accept the call."

"I accept the call of my free will."

Thomas raised his sword. "Bonded witches, bring forth your sister."

Lavina was tall and Maeve had to stand on her tiptoes to see over her shoulder.

"Come, Sister," Lavina said.

In front of Edana, Colleen stood. Any moment now, she would lead Edana to Roderick for the bonding to begin. The last bonding had happened before Maeve and many of the other witches there had been born. A deep sensation ran through Maeve's middle, hot and forceful, and her breath hitched.

Neither Colleen nor Edana moved.

Rowena nudged Maeve, hard enough to bruise her ribs.

"What?" Glaring at her, Maeve rubbed her ribs.

Rowena jerked her head to Lavina. "It's you."

Hand outstretched, Lavina stared down at her. "Come, Sister."

5

CRÉ-WITCH CHRONICLES

A round their circle, the other bonded witches were all looking at her. Even Colleen.

Maeve glanced behind her.

"Go on," Rowena urged.

Spectators on either side of her dropped back and left Maeve standing alone in front of Lavina.

Lavina was looking at her and holding her hand out like she wanted Maeve to come with her, and all Maeve could manage was a strangled, "Eh?"

"Maeve." Lavina smiled. "It's you."

"Eh?" And she really wished she could manage something better, but everybody was staring at her, and the achy, hot feeling in her belly was getting stronger.

Her gaze locked on Thomas and he motioned her forward. "My brother awaits."

"But..." She made a truncated gesture toward Edana.

Gripping her hand, very firmly, Lavina led her forward.

The prickle of all those eyes made Maeve sweat.

Edana was weeping and glowering all at once and she didn't look so pretty now.

Fiona had her arm around Edana and was whispering to her.

"It can't be me," Maeve said to Lavina. "You must be mistaken."

"Goddess does the choosing." Lavina led her to the center of the arena.

The hot feeling grew uncomfortable as it spread to her extremities. It felt like an army of red ants marching beneath her skin.

They stopped in front of Roderick.

Roderick's gaze snapped down to her. He lowered his voice and spoke softly. "Blessed."

"Coimhdeacht?" This all felt like one of her spirit walks, but not. "I don't understand."

"Trust me," he said.

Thomas took Roderick's sword and sheathed it with his own in his belt. He stepped behind Roderick and grabbed the neck edges of Roderick's robe. He ripped the robe in two and dropped the pieces to the arena floor.

Heat flooded Maeve's cheeks. She kept her gaze locked on Roderick's face.

"Naked and unarmed you stand before your witch." Thomas raised his voice so everyone could hear.

"Naked and unarmed I am before her," Roderick said.

Maeve's eyes watered with the temptation to look down.

As one, the other coimhdeacht raised their swords.

Thomas raised his. "Answer with care, Brother." He looked at Roderick. "Your word is your bond."

Roderick nodded, "My word is my bond."

"Arm yourself, Brother." Thomas handed Roderick his sword.

"I stand armed before her."

Swords raised, all the coimhdeacht turned to the north.

"Under a new moon, through the long death of winter, do you raise your sword in the power of earth to serve?"

Roderick turned with them. "My spirit joined with hers. My life for hers. From this day forth."

The coimhdeacht shifted to face east and raised their swords. "Under a waxing moon, in the glorious rebirth of spring, do you raise your sword in the power of air to serve."

A big man, Roderick flowed as gracefully as a dancer as he turned to face east. "My spirit joined with hers. My life for hers. From this day forth."

Facing south, they asked, "Under a full moon, through the deep fecundity of summer, do you raise your sword in the power of fire to serve?"

Maeve wasn't entirely sure what fecund meant, but Roderick seemed fine with it because he answered again, "My spirit joined with hers. My life for hers. From this day forth."

This couldn't be happening to her. Roderick's back was to her now and the umber marks all the coimhdeacht wore glowed beneath his skin.

With a final turn to the west, the coimdeacht asked, "Under a waning moon, through the wondrous bounty of autumn, do you raise your sword in the power of water to serve?"

Once more, Roderick said, "My spirit joined with hers. My life for hers. From this day forth."

He lowered his head and pressed his forehead to the flat of his blade. More marks scrolled across his skin, covering his arm and spilling over his shoulder and partway down his back.

Her insides felt molten.

Roderick turned and faced her. He handed his sword to Thomas and held out his hand to her.

Before she could question, Maeve took it. Sparks shot up her arm—red, yellow, blue and green, all four elements at work —and stole her breath.

Along Roderick's arm the umber marks of his calling as coimhdeacht rippled and flared.

Fascinated, Maeve touched them with the forefinger of her free hand. Power pulsed from the marks, male in origin and ancient feeling. The power spread from the point of contact and rippled through her. "They're alive."

"Aye." Roderick's voice deepened as his clasp on her hand tightened. "They respond to you."

Maeve glanced up and away again. The blaze in Roderick's eyes made her itch beneath her skin. "It's not supposed to be me."

"I'm sure that it is you." Roderick smiled.

Roderick rarely smiled but when he did, it made him impossibly handsome. Lines radiated from the corners of his eyes and bracketed his mouth. It softened the harsh lines of his face and made him as near to approachable as a five-hundred-year-old being could be.

"I'm to be bonded to you." Roderick's grip on her hand tightened.

Maeve shook her head. "No, you aren't."

"Yes, I am." Roderick raised a brow. "Goddess has decreed it as such."

"Ah, no she hasn't." Maeve winced for expressing her doubt in Goddess. Maeve didn't know how, but clearly Goddess had made a mistake.

"Yes, she has." Roderick spoke slowly and patiently as if addressing a slow child. "You're my next witch and I'm coimhdeacht to you."

"Uh-uh." She was the coven spirit walker. She barely left the caverns. She had no need for the guardianship and protection of a coimdeacht. "You must have heard her wrong."

"Maeve." He sighed and took her hand back. "Feel it."

Callouses roughened the pads of his hand as he enfolded

her smaller hand completely. Her head barely reached his shoulder.

Her fingers tingled and then her palm. Her magic woke to Goddess magic and glowed within her chest. Warmth spread outward from her chest, while the tingling in her hand moved up her arm. Her voice was a mere whisper, "What is it?"

"The bond." Roderick's jaw clenched. "Hold on tight to me. This smarts."

"Wh—"

The power in her arm crashed into the magic radiating from her chest and squeezed the air out her body.

Roderick gripped her other hand, tight enough to make her cry out, but no pain could compare to the heat and light conflagration burning through her muscles and spreading to her extremities.

The hair on her nape lifted as two streams of magic, Roderick's and hers, tangled around each other and grew stronger. Thoughts not her own flooded her mind in a dazzling flash of image after image. She had two sets of memories. She had two hearts, both beating in time with each other, two pairs of lungs laboring into one unified rhythm. Her body felt weightier, stronger, male.

Light shone from Roderick's eyes, brighter than the sun and painful to look at. Her eyes felt as if they were melting within their sockets.

The force within her built and built until it threatened to split her skin and explode in a shower of light across the arena. Through it all Roderick remained her anchor. Without him she would be cast adrift in the magic and it would burn her alive.

Her heart felt as if it would stop beating. Her lungs couldn't draw in sufficient air.

And then it all stopped.

Maeve's knees buckled and Roderick caught her against his chest.

"Breathe." His large hand stroked her back. "You're well."

Just because Roderick said so didn't make it true. Her stomach felt as if it might revolt at any moment, and her legs still refused to hold her. "What the hell was that?"

She was very much afraid she knew, but until he said those fateful words, she could still deny it.

"The bond," Roderick said, and shattered her pretense. "We're bonded."

Maeve couldn't stop staring at him. "But what am I supposed to do with that?"

6

Yesterday, Maeve had bonded a coimhdeacht, and now he was crouched at the entrance of the caverns, guarding her. Guarding her from what, she couldn't fathom. It was a bit like having a large, unfriendly dog on your heels.

The rhythmic *shrick shrick shrick* of whetstone on steel rose in counterpart to the hiss and suck of the sea far below them. She could barely concentrate with that noise.

"You know one of the wardens can do that faster." She had no idea what to say to him even. "A warden like Edana, for instance."

"I'm aware." Roderick glanced up. The onshore breeze tangled his raven-dark hair. "And Edana is no longer your concern."

Details, she needed them all, especially ones that might or might not involve a thwarted Edana. "Edana—"

"Is not your concern." He bent his head to his task again.

That was it?

She reached tentatively through the bond and found him there, a calm, determined presence, essentially male and strong. From this day forth neither of them would experience an emotion the other didn't feel, have a thought the other couldn't discern. Even their memories would be open to each other if they so chose.

Here was her chance to find out everything she wanted to know about Roderick, first and most powerful of the warrior protectors of the cré-witches, and she had no one to share her discoveries with.

Conversely the details of her rather sheltered and boring existence were his for the taking. She wished him well of the tedium. Not a salacious or interesting memory anywhere.

They barely knew each other and now they shared a bond more intimate than lovers. Could he look around her head and see her naked? "Umm…Roderick?"

He looked up.

"How does this work?" She gestured between them. "Between us, I mean. Are there rules? Things I shouldn't do? Things I should pretend I don't see or feel or hear?"

Setting aside his sword, he stood. "There won't be many secrets between us. Considering we are part of each other."

She begged herself not to giggle. That sounded oddly intimate.

"Maeve." He slid his sword into its scabbard and approached her. "I'll always be able to sense you, but we can turn the bond to a low murmur."

That was a relief. "How?"

"There are ways. Build an imaginary wall. Keep your thoughts focused on something else. Think of nothing." A brief smile twisted his mouth. "Which is going to be hard for you with the way your mind flits about."

"My mind doesn't flit."

Roderick chuckled and leaned closer. "Like a butterfly. Also, try not to shut me out too often. I'm useless to protect you if I don't know what is happening to you and you won't always have the foresight to know you're in danger."

"Huh." Which brought her back to the senselessness of their bond. "But I'm never in danger. I don't understand this."

He turned and strode away. "Ours isn't to understand why. Come along, Blessed. It's time for dinner and you're hungry."

"No, I'm not."

Roderick stared at her.

Maeve's stomach growled.

With a knowing smirk he strode through the arched doorway into the cavern beyond.

"Bossy mule of a man," she whispered, but really, really softly. Before she had merely been intimidated by Roderick, now she was fairly certain she didn't like him. Not complete dislike, yet, but edging into the wanting to smack him with something territory.

"You'll get used to me," he called. "You'll have a lifetime to do so."

Lucky, lucky Maeve.

They climbed the ancient stone staircase cleaved to the side of the cliff. No railing guarded the open side of the staircase and it would be a sheer drop some six hundred feet to the sharp boulders hemming the edge of the beach. Habit had her trailing her fingers on the rock face, but she'd made this climb too many times for it to hold much fear for her.

The staircase ended in a door built into the highest part of a stone wall. The wall ran along the bailey's sea-facing edge and disappeared into the impregnable crags that guarded Baile. Beneath the crags, the land fell away in a series of steep grassy slopes that formed a horseshoe bay beneath the castle. Accessible only from the castle above, and from the labyrinthine caverns beneath Baile Castle, the small beach appeared only at low tide. Ideal for moonlit rituals they kept secret from the village, and nightly trysts a witch wanted to keep secret from the castle. Not that Maeve had ever trysted, and now that seemed an even remoter possibility with her newly acquired hulking shadow.

She followed Roderick's broad, chain-mail-covered back. He probably slept in his hauberk, because Maeve had rarely seen him without it.

Roderick opened the arched wooden door into the bailey and paused.

"Something is amiss." Maeve stopped beside him and looked about them. A pall hung over the normally cheerful, busy bailey. On a mild evening such as this one, there should have been plenty of laughter and chatter. A keep inhabited by more than ninety women seldom remained silent.

Even the chickens Grania had fed near the well pecked silently at their feed.

The air felt wrong. The sort of wrong Maeve was coming to recognize.

Roderick pointed. "There."

A group of her sisters stood on the battlements, whispering to each other and pointing.

Cold dread slithered down Maeve's spine.

Striding ahead of her, Roderick looked over the heads of the gathered witches. He stilled before turning and blocking her path. "You don't need to see this."

"What is it?" Maeve ducked around him.

On the low rocky promontory below the castle, a group of men stood beside a newly constructed gibbet.

"Baile Castle!" One of the men turned their way and shouted up, "We want to show you what happens to witches."

In front of the men, stood three women with their hands bound behind their backs. Maeve's knees gave and she would have collapsed if Roderick hadn't caught her.

"Those three women, I know them." Maeve forced herself to look again.

"Is it your sewing circle?" His face creased in concern.

Molly was crying, Jane looked resigned and Rebecca terrified.

Maeve gripped Roderick's hand. "You have to do something. Those are my friends."

"I—"

"Maeve!" Fiona marched onto the battlements, Edana in her wake. Her face looked grim and her jaw was set in a determined line. "You can't interfere."

Thinking she couldn't have heard right, Maeve stared at Fiona. "But I know them." Perhaps Fiona hadn't realized she knew them. "They are my friends."

"They're village women," Edana sneered.

"Yes, they are." Fiona's tone gentled. "And because of that, I have no say in this matter."

Shouting, a man in a black frock coat read from a scroll. "We have tested them and found them guilty of witchcraft and consorting with the devil."

Other men placed nooses around Jane's, then Rebecca's, and finally, Molly's necks.

"You have to stop them," she begged Roderick. He was strong enough to stop what was happening.

"This is none of your affair, Coimhdeacht," Fiona snapped. "Especially after what you told me about the passed witches sending such disturbing portents. I act for the coven's safety."

Roderick's fury leaked through the bond to her. "My witch is my first and only duty."

"Only as it pertains to her safety." Fiona met his gaze and held it. "As far as this goes, you obey me."

The men were nailing a sign up above the gibbet.

"You can't mean to let them die." Maeve grabbed Fiona's sleeve. "They've done nothing wrong."

"This is none of my business." Fiona freed her sleeve from Maeve's grip. "This is village law and I can't interfere." She motioned the horrific scene before them. "Do you think this is any different from what is happening all over? Innocent women are being hung for witchcraft."

"Exactly." Maeve needed to get to her friends. She tried to get past Fiona but the coven leader grabbed her shoulders.

"Think, Maeve. If you go now, what chance do you have of saving them? None." Fiona shook her. "And you'll give the village all the excuse they need to attack us. Imagine what would happen if men like that got into Baile."

"But they won't." Maeve struggled to free herself. Fiona was surprisingly strong. "The wards protect us."

"I can't take that chance with coven lives." Fiona looked beyond her to Roderick. "Restrain her or I will."

"You can't mean to let this happen." Roderick put firm, but gentle, hands on her shoulders and drew her back. "This is tantamount to murder. I won't allow it."

"Will you break your sacred promise, Coimhdeacht?" Something dark and frightening flickered over Fiona's face.

"My first duty is to Maeve." Roderick held his ground and hope flared in Maeve.

Shaking her head, Fiona gestured her. "Yet, here she stands in no danger. The lore is clear. First your bonded witch and then the coven."

Roderick swore.

"Please." Maeve would beg on her knees if it would help.

Muscle bunched in Roderick's jaw. "My word is my bond."

"But they'll die." The words rode sobs Maeve couldn't stop. "If we don't help them, they'll die."

Fiona reached for her. "Calm yourself, Maeve. There's nothing we can do."

"You can't do this." Roderick's struggle played across his face. "You have no right."

"I have every right." Fiona looked over the battlements and

paled. "A right given to me by the coven, and my first duty is to them."

Edana looked over the battlements and winced. "There's nothing you can do for them now, in any case."

Maeve ran to the battlement and dug her fingers into the rock to keep from screaming. Above her friends, their spirits rose and hovered. And then they found their way beyond and disappeared. The tiny spirit of Jane's unborn baby rose and disappeared last.

Too enraged to face Fiona, she forced herself to look at the gibbet.

Three figures dangled poppet-like. Maeve's mood plummeted and dark anger filled her. Three women had died, and the cré-witches bore the weight of that shame.

Roderick stopped and looked. A sharp spike of anger vibrated down the bond.

"They shouldn't have died," Maeve said. She felt numb inside. It didn't help that she knew death wasn't an ending, but merely a transition. Her friends hadn't known that, and they had died in terror. "We should never have stood by while that happened."

The hanging bodies twirled in a macabre jig with the onshore breeze. Their skirts flapped like sails against their ankles.

But for Fiona, her friends might have been saved. They were the cré-witches, blessed of Goddess, and united in their purpose. Except for this.

A crow landed on the upright of the gallows and cawed loudly to his gathering murder.

"We are powerless to help them now, Blessed." Roderick's hand, warm on her arm surprised her. "We must save our fight for what we can change."

"We should have fought harder for them." The murdering

village men drifted away from their crime. Only one still stood there, tall and broad and staring up at the battlements.

The stench of the lost one rode the breeze and dark smudges appeared behind the tall figure.

Roderick stiffened. "Maeve?"

Even from this distance the malevolence eked from him. She stood transfixed.

"Maeve." Fury leaked through their bond and Maeve glanced at Roderick. His face set, he glowered at the distant figure. "In your secret monthly visits to the village, did you perhaps encounter Alexander?"

7

M aeve felt raw inside and she had returned to the caverns rather than face the hall. She would have loved to have wept, but her grief was locked in a hard, enraged tangle in her chest. It hurt to draw breath. "You knew I went to the village."

"Of course." Roderick looked grim as he paced the caverns. "Nothing happens in Baile I don't know about."

"And you never said anything?"

He folded his arms. "You weren't doing any harm, and I believed you were safe."

"Not anymore?" Whatever had him stirred up inside was like salt on the raw wound of watching her friends die.

"Not if you met Alexander. Did you?"

His imperious tone infuriated her, and she refused to be barked at. "Who is he?"

"When did you meet?"

Maeve gave up with a growl of frustration. "I didn't meet him." She briefly described her encounter. "That was the first and last time I saw him."

"Given that, he might not have been in the village that long."

"Who is he?" Maeve used a more forceful tone. If Roderick knew something about what had happened to Jane, Rebecca and Molly, then she wanted to know what that was.

Roderick looked at her, his expression inscrutable. "Alexander is Rhiannon's son."

Fear coursed through Maeve at the sound of the lost one's name spoken aloud, and she glanced about her. "She had a son?"

"Yes, there's a prophecy about the daughter of life and the son of death bearing fruit that will shape all magic to come."

"I've never heard of that." And Maeve learned all sorts of details in her spirit walks. Thoughts and memories of passed witches often lingered in the spirit realm.

Roderick shrugged. "Nobody's really sure what it means, and its existence is only known to a few."

"Alexander is the son of death?" It wasn't a far stretch to see that. The way he reeked of wrong and those awful shadows tethered to him.

"That bitch is wagering her future on him being the son of death." Roderick shook his head. "She believes he is, and she likes to keep a close eye on him. Wherever he is, she won't be far behind."

Maeve's world tilted, and she had to sit down. "You think she's behind what's happening in the village?"

"I think it would be dangerous to ignore the possibility. Just because we banished her, doesn't mean Rhiannon's bid for power is over. She was ever ambitious." Roderick looked grimmer by the moment. "This is how she works. Rhiannon spreads her malice and lets normal people act on it."

Maeve wished he would stop using that name. It made her want to bathe in the Goddess Pool to remove the taint.

Stilling, Roderick looked at the cavern walls. "You can walk with any departed witch, correct?"

"Yes." Maeve didn't know what he was staring at. The sigils looked the same as they always did.

"Even the first?"

Maeve had never attempted to walk far enough back in time to contact them. "I suppose I could."

"We need information," Roderick said. "And if that bitch is up to something, they will know it."

"They will?"

"Aye." Roderick nodded. "They were alive together for hundreds of years, even before she betrayed them. They broke her connection to Goddess magic, but they can still sense her. If she's here, then we need to know about it."

Maeve fetched her carnelian anchoring crystal and placed it at the southern edge of the pool. A walk that far back required more magic than she'd ever attempted to wield, and nerves tightened her belly.

"So, how does this work?" Roderick watched her as she gathered a pile of wood.

For a spell this powerful, she would need a lot of strength. "I'm going a long way back in time. You're going to need to keep feeding the fire when I'm beyond." After lighting the fire, she drew the ingredients she would need out of the chest she kept concealed behind a rocky ledge.

"Is it dangerous?"

"I'm not certain." Nobody had ever observed her spirit walking. Now she had Roderick trying to follow her into the place of the dead and wave his sword around.

He added a log to the blaze. "When you're in this place..."

"The spirit realm."

He picked up her bag of cleansing sage and sniffed it. "Aye, the spirit realm. I won't be able to reach you."

"No, you won't." Collectors, as spirit walkers were also called, worked alone.

"Then how will I know if you're in trouble and need me?"

"You won't." Roderick's hovering unnerved her. "The only way you'll know if I'm in trouble is if I don't come back."

Roderick's dark brows crashed over his eyes. "Don't come back?"

"Well, lose my way back and stay beyond...die." As much time as she spent with death and the dead, she should be more comfortable with that word.

"Nay." Roderick folded his arms. "I don't like it. We'll get the information another way."

"How?" She met and held his stern stare. "This was your idea, and you're right. If what you suspect is true, then we need to be forewarned."

"It was my idea and I withdraw it." His frown got even more ferocious and he looked even larger and more intimidating than before. "Your safety is my reason for being."

"I understand that." She felt too dead inside to reassure him. "But three people I valued died today. Good women who should still be alive, and if contacting the first three can help me understand why, and prevent this from happening to anyone else, then I'm going to try."

His expression grew thoughtful. Then he crouched beside her at the pool and sunk his hand beneath the water.

Nothing happened for a moment, and then the water faded from blue to silver and grew more opaque.

"Roderick," Goddess spoke, her voice a whisper that filled the caverns and resonated off the walls. Her tone grew petulant. "Where have you been? It has been too long since we have spoken."

"Your pardon, my lady." Roderick bowed his head to the water. "But I have done as you guided and bonded the spirit walker Maeve."

Maeve had never heard anyone, not even Fiona, speak so freely with Goddess.

"Good boy," Goddess purred. "You never disappoint me."

"Only there is a slight problem, my lady," Roderick said.

Goddess's tone cooled. "There are no problems in my perfect design."

"Of course not." Roderick raised an eyebrow at the churning water. "Maeve needs to spirit walk and I can't protect her in the shadow realm."

"That is not why she needs you," Goddess said. "You will be able to keep her within the bond, but your real task has not yet begun."

The water turned back to its normal iridescent green, and Roderick sighed. "That was a nonanswer."

"True." It may have been his idea that she go, but she was doing it now.

Roderick dropped his chin to his chest. "I still don't like it."

Maeve bowed her head and whispered the prayer of protection, "Goddess, beneficent and benign, walk with me now amongst all blessed who came before, all blessed who now are, and all blessed yet to come."

The sigils began a low hum, more of a vibration than an actual sound. The fire flared as she drew her birth element within.

Roderick cocked his head and stared around him at the softly glowing crystals embedded in the rock.

Goddess sent her protection, a presence pressing against Maeve's awareness, ancient and comforting.

He sniffed the air. "Oranges? And something flowery."

"Lilies." Maeve placed herbs beside her wooden bowl.

Roderick crouched beside her. "What are you doing?"

"I'm going a long way back, and it makes me more vulnerable than normal." She showed him each ingredient as she added it to the bowl. "St John's Wort for divination, bay leaves help with clairvoyance, sandalwood will open my senses to those passed and finally, frankincense will cleanse the sacred space I create."

Maeve stood and pulled fire to her. The flame danced gleefully over her outstretched palm, its touch as familiar and comforting as an old blanket.

She poured the herbs into the flame. It leaped toward them and consumed them hungrily. The flame in her hands flared higher, sending black shadows dancing over the cavern walls.

Raising her hands, she pushed the flame through the carnelian. Fire transformed into a beam of light. Lily and orange intensified as her magic molded the red light into a tunnel. Her sense of beyond opened. The hair at her nape stood on end.

The air thickened and her breathing deepened. Her heartbeat slowed. The red corridor swirled lazily and firmed into a long corridor of pure light.

Focusing on who she needed to find, Maeve stepped into the corridor. Her belly lurched and her senses swam as she accustomed herself to becoming insubstantial, intangible.

Maeve stepped out of the tunnel into a grove. Voices whispered around her.

"Sister."

"Welcome, Sister."

"Sister, come."

Passed witches surrounded her, flit through the trees. Verdant grass was velvet soft beneath her feet. Time had no place there, and she followed the path deeper. The grove thickened into a forest filled with passed witches. Their spirits brushed against her like cobwebs.

"Come." Still deeper the presence called her.

Maeve followed the summoning. The trees had grown so tall they blocked out all the light.

Stronger now, compelling and undeniable, the presence called her deeper still. *"We are here."*

The further she walked, the denser the forest got. Towering oak, rowan, hazel, holly, elder, alder, ash and birch surrounded her. Ivy twined its way up their thick trunks. Tree trunks grew so close she could barely move through them. The weight of so many thousands of spirits pulling at her made her heavy.

"Come."

She pushed into a clearing. Willow and reeds ringed a pool of dark water.

"Maeve." A woman dressed in a red gown stepped into the clearing. "It is good that you are come."

"Tahra." Maeve named the ancient guardian witch.

She was lovely with night-black hair floating and swirling around her head. Her eyes were a blue so deep it appeared indigo. Tahra stopped and cocked her head. A slow smile spread over her generous mouth. "Roderick." She stepped closer to Maeve and drew in a long breath. "I sense his bond with you."

"Yes, Ancient." Maeve was overawed.

"Sister." A second woman entered the clearing and demanded her naming.

Maeve let lily and orange swell and tell her what she needed to know, to draw from the sigils the identity of the new phantom. Another of the first four. "Brenna?"

A tall woman with brown hair and eerily opaque green eyes, Brenna had been the first seer.

Maeve's skin prickled with the power of another spirit. She almost couldn't believe it as her magic identified the third member of the first. The original healer Deidre joined the other two.

"Deirdre." Maeve bowed to them, the venerable witches whose names had been taught to every acolyte, the first witches called into service and the source from which the order of cré-witches had sprung.

"You must act," Brenna said. "The coven is in danger. The lost one has revealed herself at last."

Fear lanced through Maeve. This was what she'd come to discover. "You're sure it's her?"

"She grows in power," Tahra said.

The drain of having moved this far back in time wore on Maeve, making her feel insubstantial and ungrounded. She drew more strength from her anchoring crystal. Her mind grappled with what they said. "She has power?"

"Aye." Her sadness materialized into a gray mist that enveloped Deidre. The mist made Maeve want to weep for the lost ancient, filled as it was with the bottomless sadness of the remaining three.

"She has found a way to draw power," Brenna said, and anger leaked dirty green into the air about Maeve. Brenna wanted to strike out at something, and that fury now filled Maeve. "She's using blood magic."

Horror made her lightheaded and Maeve almost retched. "Are you certain?"

"We have seen it and we feel it." Brenna shook her head. "She strikes at the coven."

"How?" Maeve's feet sunk into the grass. Ivy twined around her ankles and tugged her deeper. She had used a lot of power to walk this deep. She was losing her connection with her anchoring crystal.

"This we can't see clearly," Deidre said. Her gaze sharpened on Maeve. "You have been here too long. You must go back."

Everything in Maeve rose in opposition to that idea. She loved it here. It was so peaceful here.

The desire to sink into the grass crept through her. The trees spread their branches toward her and surrounded her.

Leaves brushed against her cheek. She could stay. She need never go back.

A pulse shot through her, strong and sure like a sun-warmed rock. No, she couldn't stay. She needed to get back. The pulse strengthened into a steady tug, like a rope fastened about her waist pulling her back.

Tahra smiled. "Ah, Roderick." She reached out as if she could stroke the link. "Mine...and now yours."

"You must stop the lost one." Brenna's eyes grew emerald and piercing. "She must be stopped, or the cré-witches are doomed. She's the one who will bring about the end. I have seen it."

Deidre floated closer. "She attacks the wards. We can feel her blood magic within them, befouling them."

Maeve sank into the grass. Tree branches twined around her.

Strong, demanding, implacable, her bond with Roderick wrapped around her and yanked. The trees blurred as he pulled her back. Faster and faster she went until everything swirled into a gray mist rushing past her. With the speed she shot past, spirits lashed her skin.

"You must stop her," Brenna's faint whisper followed her.

And even fainter, Tahra said, "Take care of Roderick for me. His spirit craves love."

The tunnel lurched around her and threw her out. The sigils wailed her loss in a sharp, bright clamor.

Maeve stumbled and would have fallen but strong arms caught her.

Her stomach rebelled against the sudden return to her now, and she nearly threw up. Breathing deep, she clung to Roderick.

The cavern floor came into clearer view and the sigils stopped ringing in her ears.

Low and deep, Roderick's voice provided another anchor. "Are you well?"

She nodded and stood.

He looked down at her and smiled. "You have immense power, little spirit walker. The caverns crackled with it."

"Not so little." Maeve drew herself up to her full five feet and nothing.

"A veritable tower." Roderick almost smiled. "What did you discover?"

"The trouble I've been warned about." Foreboding enveloped her and her strength drained out of her. "It's already here."

8

CRÉ·WITCH CHRONICLES

Maeve woke in the hushed still of early dawn. The moment before the sun crested the horizon, in which the world held its breath for the appearance of the new day. A lone dove gurgled from the rooftop nearby. Wild streaks of coral and rose rouged the eastern sky.

Memories of the day before crashed into her and banished her appreciation of the morning.

She had a vague memory of Roderick carrying her to her chamber and putting her abed. And abed was where she wanted to stay. Until the horror of yesterday, and the fear of what was to come all went away.

A shadowy form stirred beside the fire and Roderick stepped into the light. "Good, you're awake." Taking hold of her blankets, he ripped them off her. "We need to let the coven know what you discovered."

"Roderick!" Maeve shrieked and snatched at the blanket. "Get away from me."

Straight faced, Roderick kept it out of her grasp. "You've been asleep for hours."

"And you're an evil, evil man." But as it didn't look like she was getting her warm blankets back anytime soon, she slid out of bed. "I don't want to speak to Fiona."

"I understand that, and I empathize." Roderick frowned. "But this is bigger than either of us wants. Baile is under a slow and concentrated attack of her wards."

"Could she know about the lost one? Would Baile know if it was her?" Maeve would never be comfortable uttering that name.

"It's possible. She knows me because I built her, but Rhiannon created the original wards. They are linked." He held a dress out to her. "Put this on. We meet with Fiona and Edana in five minutes."

He must have arranged the meeting while she slept. As much as she recognized she was being unreasonable, his assumption that she would fall into line annoyed her. Bitterness leaked into her tone. "Do you think Fiona will care about this?"

Roderick's expression softened infinitesimally, but she more sensed his understanding through the bond than read it on his face. "I'm not sure." He tilted her chin up to face him. "Will you trust me in this?"

Their bond was so new, and she really didn't know him. Alone had become habitual. Safe. Now she was intrinsically connected to another person, and she hadn't quite caught up with the change. Her anger against Fiona hadn't faded, but the lost one was amongst them, and if she didn't warn the coven, more deaths could follow. "I need to dress."

"Get on with it then." He folded his arms.

The man had taken leave of his senses. "You need to leave so I can get dressed."

"Really, Maeve." He gave a very male huff of exasperation. "There is nothing you have that I have not seen before."

The entire coven knew how much he'd seen. "Well, you haven't seen mine."

"God's balls." He studied her from top to toe. "I'll stand outside, but no going back to bed. You have three minutes."

No, she sodding well didn't. "Boor," she whispered at his departing back.

Not for a king's ransom would she meet with Edana feeling like she'd been dragged through a hedge backward.

Maeve dressed in her best gown, nothing like Edana's gold gown, but the blue went well with her eyes, and it displayed her neat waist and hugged her bosom. She braided her hair and joined Roderick outside her chamber.

He straightened from where he had been leaning on the wall. "We're late."

"I'm not late," she said, but part of her knew she was taking her anxiety at seeing Fiona and Edana out on him. She hated that she had to have this meeting. "Because I didn't set the time."

"Blessed!" He grabbed her arm and stopped her. "We can't be at odds, you and I."

"Coimhdeacht!" She looked up to meet his gaze. "Then you need to discuss things with me and not decide them on my behalf."

"Fine." He gritted his teeth. "Now, come along. What you discovered won't wait."

He led her to Fiona's quarters.

Edana must have moved in because she lounged in the sitting room beside the fire. She rose in a graceful movement that Maeve could spend her lifetime practicing and still blunder through and held her hands to Roderick. She smiled up at him and batted her lashes "Roderick."

"Edana." He took her hands, for no longer than politeness dictated, and dropped them again.

The way Edana looked at him set Maeve's teeth on edge. Given her way, Edana would gobble him up. "I'm here to see Fiona."

"You're late." Edana raked Maeve with a harsh glare. Maeve was suddenly aware how short she was, and how her mouth was a tad too large for beauty, and of the eighteen freckles over the bridge of her nose.

"Your pardon, Blessed." Roderick drew Edana's attention back to him. "I was detained, and the fault is mine."

Maeve almost forgave him the crack about her having nothing he hadn't seen before.

Sniffing, Edana strode to the door at the end that led into the office. "She does not have much time for you. There is more trouble."

"From the village?" Maeve's gut tightened. She prayed no more deaths.

Edana frowned at her. "I can't share coven business with just any witch."

"Maeve lost three friends yesterday." Roderick's harsh tone stopped Edana in her tracks. "More than anyone, she deserves to know if she will lose more before something is done."

"Of course, she does," Edana simpered and laid a hand on his arm. "Forgive me. This awful business has none of us thinking straight."

Maeve suppressed a snort. "The village?"

Edana spoke to Roderick. "The village has sent a list of what it calls devil worship and acts against God. It has given us five days to respond."

"What will Fiona do?" Roderick asked for both of them.

Edana shrugged. "What can she do? We are witches, but we don't worship the devil. To them those two things are one and the same." She lifted her chin. "They can send all the nasty missives they want, however, because those won't get them past the wards."

Maeve glanced at Roderick. She didn't share Edana's blithe confidence, especially not after her spirit walk last night. "We need to see her."

"I said you could, and you will. Do you think you're the only sister who wishes to speak with Fiona?" Edana drew herself up, her beautiful face cold and disdainful. "I'm only allowing you to speak to her as a favor to Roderick."

Goddess led the cré-witches, not Fiona and certainly not Edana. "As a sister, it's my right to see Fiona when I need to."

"Really?" Edana didn't look so pretty with her face all screwed up in a nasty grimace. "Now that you have him, I see you have grown a backbone."

"I don't have him." Maeve's cheeks heated. "He bonded me."

"He was supposed to bond me."

"Edana." Roderick stepped between them. "I have no say in who I bond, and Maeve's news must not wait."

"You bonded Tahra, and she was your lover." Edana looked on the verge of tears.

Roderick flushed and averted his gaze from her. "Being lovers had nothing to do with it."

"You should have bonded me." Edana glared at Maeve, as if she had somehow done something to make Roderick bond with her.

Maeve smirked, girl enough to enjoy her moment of triumph.

Fiona opened her office door. "Maeve. And Roderick. Come in."

She shut the door on a gawking Edana.

"Maeve." Fiona winced. "You must hold me to blame for the death of your friends." Tears filled Fiona's large brown eyes. "In truth, I hold myself to blame as much as if I had driven a dagger into their hearts."

The words were right, as was Fiona's expression. Maeve couldn't account for the faint metallic tang on her tongue, or her skin prickling. The words she should have spoken stuck in her throat.

"Coven leader." Roderick stepped between them and took Fiona's hands. His voice deepened like warm, rich cream. "To be a leader sometimes demands difficult decisions. My bond-mate still mourns the loss of her dear friends, but she will come to see that you acted out of the best interests of the coven."

Like bloody hell she would.

Roderick shot a repressive pulse of emotion through the bond. He followed that with a blanketing wave of reassurance. He was asking her to keep her tongue and trust him. As she certainly didn't trust Fiona farther than she could toss her, she kept silent.

Fiona's voice shook. "Thank you, Roderick. But the death of those three women is mine to bear, as is Maeve's anger."

"Fiona." Maeve dredged up a conciliatory tone. She must have leached it from Roderick, because she wasn't feeling that way at all. "We must put that aside. We have a bigger problem."

Eyes wide, Fiona turned to her. "What can you mean?"

"The spirits are disturbed and last night I made contact with the first." Even with the door shut, Maeve lowered her voice. "It's the lost one." Saying it aloud made her shiver. Rhiannon, the lost witch, the dark witch. "They say she's back."

"You know—" Fiona started. "What did they say?"

"The ancients have seen her." Dread crept through Maeve. "They say she rises in power and she's using blood magic."

"Blood magic?" Fiona paled. "How would the ancients know? Are they sure? Are you sure?"

Yes, to all of Fiona's questions. "I am."

"And the ancients are sure it's her? You're sure you're not mistaken in this?"

Fiona's response bothered her, but she couldn't put her finger on why. As spirit walker, Maeve had access to all the knowledge of witches past and future. She could walk amongst souls not on this physical plane. Why would Fiona doubt she or the witches passed spoke the truth? "I walked with them, all three of them. They can feel her blood magic and it terrifies them. Deidre told me she attacks the wards."

"Oh, my!" Fiona blinked at them. "This is most unexpected."

"They have urged me to act," Maeve said.

Fiona glanced from Maeve to Roderick and sighed. "Very well! Thank you for telling me this, Sister. You did well to bring it to me."

"Will you tell the wardens to strengthen the wards?" Maeve followed Fiona to the door. "They should be able to pick up the blood magic."

"I need to think on it." Fiona took Maeve's hand and squeezed it. "I must ask you not to say anything to our coven sisters about any of this. We wouldn't want them to worry."

"Shouldn't we all be worried?" Blessed didn't keep secrets from each other. If her sisters' lives were threatened, they deserved to know.

Fiona frowned. "Of course you're right. But there is only so much bad news one can deal with at once." She rubbed her temple. "I only ask you to keep this to yourself for a day or two. Until I can think what must be done."

"But I—"

"Of course, Blessed." Roderick took Maeve's elbow. When she opened her mouth to argue further, he tightened his grip and said, "We'll say nothing until you do. Like you, I think it wise not to cause panic."

He all but dragged Maeve out of the office and through the small sitting area. A party of healers stood with Edana, and they looked distressed.

When they were almost back to her bedchamber, Maeve wrenched her arm free. "Why did you do that?"

Roderick raised his hand and opened her door. He ushered

her in and shut the door before he spoke again. "What I'm doing is irrelevant. The better question, Blessed, is why do I suspect that Fiona already knew about Rhiannon?"

9

The next morning, Roderick charged into her chamber when her eyes were barely open. "The amount of time you spend in that bed makes me think you want me to join you there."

"Really?" She had countless years ahead of being woken similarly. Oh, the unrestrained joy! "Or is that not perhaps because you spend so much time leaping from bed to bed that this is where your thoughts take you?"

He grinned. "Get dressed. You missed breakfast and the furor in the hall."

Missing breakfast was normal for her. Dead witches didn't care what time of day or night it was; when they wanted her attention, they made sure she knew it. "What furor?"

Roderick grunted and stared at her. "You didn't sleep last night."

"Were you spying on me?" They needed to set some rules of engagement.

His flat stare was the Roderick equivalent of an eye roll. "Why would I need to spy on you when I have you rattling around in my head?"

He had a point, and she settled for a dismissive glare as she washed her face. "Tell me about the furor."

Roderick hesitated, but so minutely she almost missed it. "The healers are angry with Fiona. They're threatening to thwart her authority."

"Why?" Thwarting would probably lead to more trouble, and the healers were a gentle lot for the most part.

"There has been a development." Roderick cleared his throat. "In the village."

Maeve's belly dropped. Please, Goddess, no more murders of innocent women. She waited for him to tell her more.

"No more hangings." He opened her bedchamber door and spoke to someone on the other side. Shutting the door, he breathed and turned to her. "It seems there is contagion within the village."

"Oh, bloody hell!" This couldn't have come at a worse time.

"Indeed." Roderick straightened his hauberk.

Maeve sat on her bed, her weak knees demanding she do so. "The healers will want to go to the village."

"It is within the nature of healers." Roderick shrugged.

Healers paid dearly for their gift. They drew the disease and hurt of others into themselves, and then transmuted it into the earth. They willingly took on the pain and illness of others and did it whenever they were needed. "They need to help," Maeve said.

A knock came at the door and an apprentice entered with a tray for Maeve. Sweetly round with big brown eyes and glossy walnut hair, the girl batted her lashes at Roderick. "Guardian." She giggled.

"Blessed." He gave her his smoldering half smile. The same one that had been wreaking havoc in girlish hearts since...probably since he'd been doing it. And as he was older than dust, that amounted to a lot of hearts fluttering. Well, he could cut that out in her chamber. She sent Roderick a repressive stare and turned it on the apprentice for good measure.

Undeterred, Roderick gave the girl a reassuring smile and ushered her out the door. "The healers have been arguing since Fiona announced her decree over breakfast."

"Decree?" Maeve stuffed her mouth with bread and cheese as she dressed.

Roderick helped himself to the tray as well. "Fiona has announced that given what happened with the hangings and the demands from the village that Baile Castle is shut. Nobody comes in and nobody goes out."

Maeve stared at him. Not only had Fiona overstepped her bounds, the healers would never accept they couldn't help allay the suffering in the village. And nor should they. It went against everything they stood for as cré-witches to hide in their castle whilst suffering went on around them. Goddess had created them to succor and protect her creation.

"We need to get to the hall." Roderick folded his arms. "If you're done stuffing your cake hole like a plowman."

Maeve took a deep breath, refusing to acknowledge his rudeness and finished dressing instead.

As she headed for the door, Roderick fell into place behind her. A big man, he made barely a sound as he followed her down the stairs towards the great hall.

The buzz of angry voices reached them from the top of the central staircase.

"The council has decided." Fiona's strident tones cut through others. "This discussion is pointless. You already know the answer to your request. You merely refuse to accept it."

Maeve winced. That wouldn't go down well.

The angry roar in response to Fiona proved Maeve right. She reached the entrance to the hall, and paused, taking in the lay of the land.

Clear divisions separated the hall. A strip of floor separated both sides of the argument physically. Unfortunately, Fiona's side appeared more populous. Surely so many of her fellow witches couldn't believe in isolation.

On the opposite side sat the healers, all of them, united in their desire to cure the sick. The bonded witches stood with the healers.

Standing close to Lavina, Thomas looked up and the look he gave Roderick was grim.

The council, arrayed at a table behind Fiona on the dais, appeared to be in complete agreement.

"The council's decisions are final." Fiona sneered and let her gaze stray over the hall. "It isn't up to any of you to question them."

Head healer, Joy, stepped to the front of the group. "You go too far, Fiona."

"We don't go far enough." Edana tossed her head. "None of us goes far enough if we sit here and tolerate this defiance."

"Tolerate?" The question escaped Maeve before she could stop it.

Ever mindful of her safety, Roderick moved closer to her.

And not a moment too soon, as all gazes in the hall swung her way.

Maeve faced Fiona. All the attention had her knees knocking and she sent them a quick reprimand. "Since when do we speak of tolerating defiance? We're not subject to each other's rule." She gave a respectful nod. "Even you're there to guide, and not to rule."

"Being bonded has given you a voice, it seems." Edana sniffed. "What a pity none of us care to hear it."

Roderick stepped in front of Maeve. "You should hear her, for so speaks the spirit walker, and we should heed her for she knows the lore better than any of us."

A mutter of agreement rose from the healers' side of the hall.

Whilst Maeve appreciated the support, the very division was wrong. Cré-witch shouldn't stand against cré-witch. They strove for harmony and balance in all they did.

"I'll grant you she can quote the lore to all of us." Edana waved an airy hand. "She could quote the lore to us until our eyes crossed with boredom."

Fiona's side of the hall chuckled.

Fiona held her hands up for silence. "Spirit walkers understand the lore only inasmuch as it pertains to the dead. They know nothing of the troubles besetting the living."

"I beg your pardon." Angry color suffused Joy's cheeks. "I would suggest that the person who knows nothing of which they speak, here today, is you."

Fiona's eyes glittered as she faced Joy. "You would say that. You would side with whoever agrees with you."

"You dare question my honesty?" Joy's voice rang across the hall.

"Indeed." Fiona drew herself up. "I dare that and a whole lot more. I do so with the very authority this coven granted me." She gestured to her side of the hall. "And I have the support of the majority of our sisters."

Joy paled and then went a dull brick red. She opened and closed her mouth, before resuming her seat.

The rest of the hall just sat there. Maeve couldn't believe they were going to let this lie.

Sheila's voice shook as she said, "You can't stop us from attending to those who need us." But her defiance sounded hollow, without substance.

Fiona thought so too, and the smile she turned on Sheila made Maeve's blood run cold.

"Do not make that mistake," Fiona said. "In this time of crisis, the council has tasked me with protecting the coven. And I'll do so by any means I deem fit."

Maeve stared at the council. Not one of them looked up from their keen scrutiny of the table in front of them.

"Then you had best prepare yourself to make good on that threat," Joy said. "Because there are people in that village who need us, and no power in this life, or the next, will stop us from giving them that help."

Fiona's eyes flashed fire. "Be careful, Sister," she said. "That sounded remarkably like a challenge."

They all felt the shift in the air as Fiona reached for her magic. A faint metallic stink underlay the mint and raspberry scent of Fiona's magic.

Shock held the hall immobile. To even think of using your magic against another witch was so forbidden it took the hall a precious moment to understand the nature of Fiona's threat.

Not Roderick, though. He already had Maeve by the arm and out of the hall. By the time she recovered enough to protest he had her halfway up the staircase, and the prickle of working magic had disappeared.

"She..." The words escaped her ability to wrestle them into order.

"Aye." Roderick looked grim. "She was ready to toast the lot of you."

"But..." No witch, not since the lost one, had or would consider breaking the second highest rule of all, a rule that had only been added because of the lost one. Maeve shuddered. Even thinking of her made Maeve cold to her middle. The lost one's conscienceless bid for power over three hundred years ago had nearly been the end of the cré-witches. It was a lesson none of them could afford to ignore.

10

CRÉ-WITCH CHRONICLES

M aeve couldn't stand by and let the villagers die. She had failed Rebecca, Jane and Molly. She wouldn't fail the other villagers. Pacing the caverns, she searched for something, anything, to help them.

To help the village meant either openly disobeying Fiona or getting to the village in secret. The idea rushed through her mind and she almost laughed. The solution was right there before her.

Roderick stepped into her path and folded his arms. "No."

"No what?" The idea had barely even taken root.

He leaned closer until they were almost nose to nose. "You aren't to lead the healers through the secret passage to the village."

"Why not?" She wanted to stamp her foot or shake the stubbornness out of him.

He jabbed a finger toward the village. "I don't care about Fiona's decree. Alexander is in that village, and I'll wager my balls so is his bitch mother. You're not going there."

"But I can sense them. If either of them reaches for their magic, I can smell it now." She needed him to understand how much it meant to her. "I'll stay away from them. I know those villagers. Some of them are my friends." Her words seemed to bounce off him. "And the villagers know the healers well. They won't betray us."

"I don't share your faith in the villagers." His face showed no emotion, but his eyes were frigid. "And I would never make the mistake of underestimating Rhiannon again. It's impossible to know how deep her rot infects the village."

"I'll be careful." She wasn't getting through to him. "Please, Roderick, I won't be responsible for more death if I can help it."

Empathy pulsed down their bond. "You're not responsible for those women dying. Fiona is."

"But I didn't do anything either." She opened the bond to show him her hurt. "This time I can act. I can stop people from dying."

Roderick shook his head. "I understand, but I can't allow it."

"Allow it?" She smacked him with an emotional blast. "Since when do you allow me to do as I want?"

Roderick lifted his sleeve and pointed to his coimhdeacht markings. "The day Goddess put these on me. They give me the right to do anything to keep you safe, including this." He drew himself up. "I forbid you going to the village."

"For—forbid me?' She could barely get the word out. "By what right?"

"By Goddess granted right." His expression hardened. "And I'm going to stay right on your heels to make sure you obey me."

He would too.

Their stalemate lasted throughout the day and into the night.

After dinner, Roderick walked her to her chamber. Once inside, he tossed a cushion on the floor and lay down by the fire.

"What are you doing?"

He rolled and presented her his back. "What does it look like I'm doing?"

"I know what it looks like." The desire to kick his perfectly shaped bum sharpened in her. "And you aren't sleeping in my chamber."

"Yes, Maeve, I am." He sat up and pinned her with a hard stare. "Right on your heels."

He lay down again.

Maeve sat on her bed a long time and stared at his back. She didn't like her chances of being able to sneak past him.

A change in strategy was needed.

Clearing her mind, she went about getting ready for bed.

Roderick's back rose and fell, and his eyes were shut.

She relented and laid a blanket over him.

"Thank you." He glanced up at her. "Go to sleep, Maeve. In the morning we can find a way to change Fiona's mind."

That was a futile task if ever she'd heard one. Fiona wasn't going to change her mind. Maeve had deep, dark suspicions about Fiona. Suspicions she didn't even want to share with Roderick yet, but beneath the normal smell of Fiona's magic, Maeve had caught the stench of blood magic.

Morning found Roderick still in her room, but now Maeve had a plan. If you couldn't go through a rock wall, over it or around it, you had to burrow beneath.

It took three days for him to relax his vigilance. Three days in which she counted the minutes that sick villagers didn't have.

He seemed to accept her compliance as his due and had been discussing options with Thomas and the other coimhdeacht. Discussion Maeve wanted to scream her frustration at but didn't. She already had the solution.

Presently, Roderick was lounging at the cavern entrance, eyes closed, and soaking up the sun.

Roderick was wrong but arguing with him was like

shouting at a stone. She knew the villagers, had met many of them during her monthly visits. They didn't all feel like those awful men.

And the village needed help, and that came before any consideration of personal safety.

As she fumed and waited, contagion galloped unchecked through the village. Already it had carried off its first victims. Last night they had gone to sleep with the sickly sweet stench of burning flesh carried on the wind. At least the villagers knew enough to burn the bodies. But there shouldn't have been any bodies. If the council had only allowed the healers amongst the villagers, they might have prevented it. They still might prevent it if bloody Roderick would take himself off for an hour or two.

Maeve had a brief, but fierce, fantasy of shoving him off the cliff edge. Although she didn't really wish him harm. Or much harm. At least not the irreparable type of harm. She merely wished he would stop being such a stubborn ass, which was akin to wishing the moon was made of gold, and thus brought her back to her shoving fantasy.

Roderick yawned and stood.

Maeve was momentarily distracted. For a big man, he moved with feline elegance.

Roderick nodded at the bailey above them. "I thought I might get in some arms practice," he said. "The coimhdeacht need to be prepared for anything."

"Because of the lost one." Maeve nodded. She agreed with him about being prepared.

"If you're sure you'll have no need of me?" Enough sarcasm laced Roderick's question to assure her that her lack of enthusiasm over his presence hadn't gone unnoticed.

Yes! Finally. If she suddenly became sweet and amenable it would raise his suspicions for sure. So, she shrugged and stuck her bottom lip out. "I'm sure I can muddle along without you."

He stared at her, none of his thoughts evident on his face.

"Everything I do," he said, "is done to protect you. Believe it or not, my intention is rarely to vex you."

"Rarely? But not never to vex me." If she'd been more in charity with him that last might have made her laugh.

He shrugged. "I'm but human. Occasionally temptation gets the better of me."

This time, he succeeded in making her laugh. "Go and play with your sword. "

"I will." He grinned at her. It wasn't something he did often, and she was glad of it. Roderick had a disconcertingly appealing smile. "I'll try not to cut anything vital."

"Don't try too hard," she called after him.

His boots scuffed against the stone stairs as he climbed to the bailey.

Keeping all thoughts out of her mind, she waited for him to disappear. Then she waited some more, until his attention shifted off her.

Her awareness of him was dim, but she could sense he wasn't concentrating on her. Keeping her thoughts deliberately blank, she ran up the stairs to the bailey. She grabbed the arm of a journeywoman hurrying past.

"Spirit Walker!" The woman jumped as if death beckoned her and her brown eyes widened. "Can I help you?"

"Yes." Maeve spoke quickly, aware that Roderick's concentration on her had intensified again. "Get a message to Sheila," she whispered. "Tell her if she and whichever healers she trusts the most wish to go to the village, they'd better get here now."

The journeywoman gaped at her, and several horrible seconds dragged past.

Roderick's questioning pulse probed at her mind, and she deflected it with a child's song. She had no idea if it would work or not, but it was all she could come up with.

Then, the journeywoman nodded. "I'll tell her."

"And make sure Roderick doesn't find out." Maeve gave her a shove.

Roderick's presence drew nearer.

Moments after the journeywoman scuttled off, he rounded the corner of the castle toward her. His shirt was flung over his shoulder and sweat beaded his belly and chest. By the love of all Goddess had created, it was a sight to behold.

A pair of apprentices stopped and stared at him. Then huddled together and giggled.

"Ladies." Roderick flashed his grin at them.

Her need to crawl all over him was replaced by the need to kick him. Maeve met his gaze and held it. "I thought you were at arms practice."

"I was." Tilting his head, he studied her from toe to tip. "But you're up to something. Something you don't want me to know about."

Maeve huffed, flapped her hands and rolled her eyes. She sniffed and tried to look innocent.

Roderick bent that pale, pale blue gaze on her and looked.

"It's nothing." She gave up with a growl. "Can't a woman have a secret or two?" Inspiration struck. "I was only going to spirit walk."

"Uh-huh." He leaned closer until their noses almost bumped. "Even if I couldn't sense you, you're a terrible liar."

"Am not." She could lie about all sorts of things. "I lie all the time about things you would know nothing about because I'm lying."

His lips quirked as if he was trying not to laugh. "I'll find out what it is."

"Hah!" She met his challenge and raised it. "There's nothing to find out."

"This functions better," he said, waving a hand between them, "if we work together and are honest with each other."

Like she would fall into line with that. "And by that you mean if I do what you say."

"If you say so." He gave her a feral grin filled with male conceit. He turned and strode away, calling over his shoulder. "I'll find you later. Best get your little mysteries out the way before I return."

He could wager his sword arm on that. Maeve returned to the caverns to wait.

Agonizing minutes crawled by. Agonizing minutes she spent constructing her emotions and thoughts into a believable stream to keep Roderick from rushing back.

At last, Sheila led four of her fellow healers into the cavern. Glancing about as if scared someone would stop her, she hurried up to Maeve. "Spirit Walker, what is this about? Do you know a way to the village?"

Her name was Maeve. Not that hard to remember when she and Sheila had grown up together.

Roderick caught her irritation and his question tapped politely on her awareness.

Maeve shrunk her emotions into a tight ball and thought the ball into a box and closed the lid. "I want to help, and I can."

"With?" Sheila glanced at her fellow healers before leaning closer to Maeve.

"The village." Maeve drew them deeper into the caverns. "There's a way to the village. It's an ancient passage, from before the castle was built." And up until very recently she'd believed she was the only one who knew of the secret passage. "I can lead you to the village and bring you back again without anyone knowing."

Sheila looked eager but nervous. "What about Roderick?"

Maeve waved a dismissive hand and bawled a child's song in her mind. "He's playing with his sword."

A witch behind Sheila sighed. "I wish I could play—"

"Right!" Sheila said. "We'll follow you."

Maeve hurried into the first cavern and skirted the Goddess Pool. The water rippled in acknowledgment of their passing. Maeve took that as a sign of her approval.

The healers followed her into the shadowy depression.

Placing both hands against the rock, Maeve muttered the incantation.

Rock shimmered and dissolved into a person–size opening.

One of the healers gasped. The rest murmured amongst themselves.

"I had no idea this was here." Sheila followed her into the dark passageway, gaze going this way and that.

"Nobody does." Maeve waited for the last healer to step into the corridor before she uttered the incantation and closed the opening behind them.

She snapped her fingers and brought four flames into being. They needed enough light to hurry along the passage. Soon Roderick would finish his arms practice and waste no time coming to find her. Baile had been his castle before the witches took him amongst them. The bond between him and the castle was as solid as the stone from which Baile was built. Maeve wasn't sure yet how it worked between Roderick and Baile, but she couldn't risk the castle telling tales on her.

Maeve hurried her party along. Once she had the healers in the village, doing what they did best, Roderick would stand no chance of getting them back within Baile Castle until they were ready.

The passageway carried them through a confusing number of turns, in which it was impossible to keep your bearings if you didn't already know the way.

The abrupt ending of the corridor always took her by surprise.

Sheila cursed and narrowly avoided running into her back.

A scuffle and a curse from further back resulted from two not-so-alert healers crashing into each other.

As she released her flames, Maeve made the opening incantation too softly for Sheila to hear much. Having the coven able to dart back and forth between village and castle was asking for trouble.

Light flooded the tunnel.

Maeve and her followers stepped into the crypt. She closed the passageway after the last witch slid through. It would never do for some enterprising young clergyman to stumble across their secret.

She took the stairs up into the churchyard, and motioned Sheila to precede her down the village road. She had gotten them there. It was time for the healers to do what they did.

11

CRÉ-WITCH CHRONICLES

The closer they drew to the village, the more dead appeared to Maeve. Spirits hung in the air, still tethered to their bodies. In cases of many sudden deaths, spirits struggled to find their path from the mortal realm.

The children's spirits were the worst. So many it broke her heart. They still wore their flesh incarnation and would soon discard that and become pure spirit, ageless, sexless, nationless, but for now they still looked like the poor babies they had so recently been.

From the burial fires, she drew her birth element. It moved sluggishly, dragging the weight of grief created by all the death. The dead turned to her, drawn by her kindred spirit.

"Mother Goddess, open the pathway," she whispered the incantation.

The healer standing nearest her shivered. "It grows chilly."

Maeve didn't have the heart to tell the woman she was presently being crossed by a number of spirits. They released the shadow of their human forms in a shower of sparks and dissolved. The transfer from one state of being to another caused the cold sensation the healer felt.

Normally Maeve arrived when the healers had done all they could. They were rarely happy to see her.

For safety's sake, the witches elected to stay in twos as they crept from home to home. Maeve stayed beside Sheila. Some villagers were surprised to see them, others so pathetically grateful, it brought tears to Maeve's eyes.

Sheila worked tirelessly, helping one person and moving to the next, barely pausing long enough to take a sip of water. In her wake, people rested comfortably, taking the sleep of healing.

Watching Sheila and providing an extra pair of hands when she needed them, was a true revelation. Maeve stopped Sheila at a cottage door. The ghost of the recently departed young man hovered. Maeve shook her head at Sheila. "Not here."

"Blast it!" Sheila took the loss as a personal affront but moved to the next cottage.

The situation in the village was so much worse than Maeve had guessed. She followed Sheila into another home.

An exhausted woman looked up as they came in. Three children lay in a bed to one side, their waxen complexions achingly familiar to Maeve.

The woman sobbed and stumbled when she saw Sheila. "Blessed." She fell to her knees. "Please, Blessed, my children."

"Your children will be seen to." Sheila bent and helped the woman into the chair. "First, however, when did you last rest?"

The woman looked confused and wiped the back of her hand over her forehead. "I...not sure. The littlest one fell sick three nights ago, the rest shortly after."

"You go." Maeve motioned Sheila to help the children. The children would live. Maeve saw their spirits within their young, struggling bodies. It wasn't their time. The kettle was hot, so she made the woman a cup of tea and brought her a bowl of the beef broth that had been simmering on the hearth. "You need to eat," she said. "You're no good to them if you collapse."

The hope in the woman's eyes almost crumpled Maeve. "They will live?" She grabbed Maeve's hand and squeezed it hard enough to bring tears to Maeve's eyes. "They will live?"

Sheila looked up sharply and frowned.

Nodding, Maeve spoke to Sheila. "They will live."

The sweetest expression crossed Sheila's face, part hope and part joy. She swallowed and bent back over the sick children.

When they left, the mother slept beside her children. The children breathed easily now and slept deeply.

Sheila hurried on and Maeve with her. They had no time to tarry.

The story was the same throughout the village, no home completely unaffected by the contagion.

Sheila stumbled and Maeve caught her elbow. "You're tired. You must stop."

"We can't help them all." Sheila swiped stray hair from her wan face. "We can only deal with the worst of them today, and pray the others survive long enough for us to return."

All five healers bore signs of growing weariness. Their magic scrolled through the air—green, yellow, red and blue as the healers used their birth elements to fuel their blessings. The signature scents of the five working healers' magic helped disguise the stench of the funeral pyres.

The number of sick was terrifying, and the witches worked to exhaustion, taking the barest minimum time to transmute the disease. And then they rid themselves of only enough so they could continue to function.

Sheila stopped suddenly and a violent coughing fit shook her. She wasn't the first witch to show symptoms of succumbing to the contagion.

Maeve grabbed her arm before she could enter a new dwelling. "You have to rest."

"No time." Sheila shook her arm free. "We can transmute

this when we return to Baile. But we need to get as many of the sick as we can."

"Sheila—"

"I don't have time for this." Sheila scowled at her. "You can't have one more soul."

Maeve winced. A lot of witches saw her as death itself. "You'll make yourself sick." Maeve's words died in the empty space Sheila had vacated.

As she ducked into the door of a small, unkempt cottage, another paroxysm of coughing shook Sheila. Worried Sheila would faint, Maeve hurried to her side, but Sheila kept moving.

It took Maeve a moment to realize whose cottage this was. It was the same one Maeve had peeped into that night she had seen the beautiful, evil Alexander.

Inside, the cottage was in disarray and smelled of sickness. Sheila hurried to Agnes's side. She looked nothing like the Agnes Maeve had seen that night. In only a few short days, the disease had ravaged the beautiful woman and left her emaciated.

"My baby." Agnes's voice rasped painfully in her throat. "Save my baby."

The small, simple wooden cradle that had sat by the hearth was now beside her bed. Someone had carved it with loving hands.

Already free of its body, the baby's spirit hovered.

Maeve's skin crawled and her hackles rose as she looked at the dead infant's spirit. It was wrong—other—in a way that reminded her of Alexander. She whispered the incantation to show the dead their pathway. The infant's spirit wavered, like a candle flickering in the wind, and stayed. It strained as if trying to reach the pathway, but something held it tethered in this realm. Maeve went to the spirit to release whatever held it bound.

The blood magic taint of the spirit coated the back of her

throat and she recoiled. This baby had been sacrificed for blood magic. Its spirit was forever separated from Goddess. This spirit would never be reborn again. Its journey was ended, but it's torment had only just begun. Unable to return and resume its journey, the spirit would still crave to do so. Each moment it existed, tethered to this plain and separated from life, it would be aware of its confinement.

She hurried back to Sheila and tugged on her sleeve. Blood magic meant the lost one and Alexander. They needed to leave.

Sheila kept her unwavering attention on the mother. "I'll see to the little one."

"My baby," Agnes whimpered. Bones protruded through the dirty parchment of her skin. Bloody sores surrounded her mouth, and fever brought the lie of a healthy flush to her cheeks. She had been so pretty that time before. "No." She batted Sheila's hands away. "My baby, you must save my baby."

Agnes had been practicing blood magic. The signs on her body were not contagion. Maeve grabbed Sheila and pulled her away. "You need to listen."

Agnes's gaze snapped to Maeve, intent and fierce. She stuck out her tongue and licked the air. "Cré-magic." She breathed deep, a blissful expression on her face. "So sweet."

Sheila leaped back from Agnes, snatching her hands to her chest. "What is that?"

"Blood magic," Maeve said. "Her baby didn't die of the plague. She used her baby's life to wield blood magic."

"Goddess save you." Sheila clapped her hands over her mouth and retched. "What have you done?"

Eyes glittering, Agnes stood. "I do my mistress's bidding." She giggled and rolled her eyes until the whites showed. "She loves the magic, craves the magic. It calls her and she comes."

Dear Goddess, there was only one being who could wield blood magic. "We have to go." Maeve pulled Sheila from the cottage.

Sheila stumbled after her, gaze stuck on the woman. "What is happening? What is she talking about?"

"The lost one." Maeve looked about her, scared to say that name out loud. "Agnes serves Rhiannon."

Sheila gaped at her and then gave a strangled little laugh. "The lost one is dead. What are you talking about?"

"She's far from dead." Suddenly, her walk with the first three made horrible, undeniable sense, and judging by the strength of the blood magic surrounding Agnes alone, it would take an intervention by Goddess herself to kill Rhiannon now. "The lost one is strong and she's wielding blood magic in this village." And that meant they were in so much trouble. "We need to get behind Baile's wards. Now."

"I don't understand." Sheila glanced toward the cottages she had yet to visit. "I need to help them. They need us."

"You can't." Maeve pulled her toward the churchyard and the tunnel entrance. If they could get behind Baile's wards, the castle would protect them. Out here, and only the six of them, they were like bait worms dangling in the water.

"Cré-witches, come and play." Agnes followed them. Fetid, cold blood magic wreathed her.

"Call your healers." Maeve stood between Sheila and Agnes. "Get them to safety."

Agnes's fixed her gaze on Maeve. "You shouldn't have interfered." She smiled, displaying a mouth of rotten teeth and bleeding gums. "But they're too late, you know. My mistress had everything in place, and nothing can stop us now. Those ancient bitches told you too late." She giggled, blood and spit trickling down her chin. "My lady will reclaim what is hers."

"Maeve." Sheila's eyes were huge. "What is she talking about?"

Maeve crowded Sheila back and away from Agnes.

A knot of villagers gathered in the road.

"Sheila." Another healer appeared beside them. "I don't

understand. Aren't we here to help them? There are still so many who need help."

Sheila dragged her horrified gaze from Agnes. "We need to go."

The youngest healer, a sweet girl called Rose, stumbled over a rock and fell to her knees. The others rushed to help her, but Rose hung limp in their hands. She tried to walk, but her legs gave out beneath her, and were it not for the two healers holding her up, she would have fallen again.

"Alexander said you would come." Agnes's face twisted into a cunning smirk, and she threw back her head and let out a tortured scream. She turned and dashed into her cottage.

The healer in Sheila warred with her fear and she took half a step toward the cottage, wanting to help Agnes, needing to ease her pain.

"You can't help her." Maeve blocked her path. "She's beyond anything a healer can do for her. Save yourselves."

Agnes's screaming grew more agonized. More people appeared in the doorways of neighboring cottages. They looked about them in confusion, their gazes lingering on the small party of cré-witches.

Dead baby clutched to her breast, Agnes burst into the roadway. "They killed her." She pointed at Sheila. "They killed my baby."

"What is this now, Agnes?" A tall matron bustled out of her cottage and headed for Agnes. Maeve had helped her say goodbye to a dead son a few months ago. "Those are the healers, from on the hill. They help us." She peered at the baby clutched to Agnes's breast and pity softened her face. "I'm sure they didn't kill your baby."

Maeve motioned her fellow cré-witches to follow her and kept backing away down the road.

Tall and broad, a man stepped into Maeve's path. The aquiline perfection of his features stopped her. He was as beautiful as the last time she had seen him, and twice as deadly. She didn't know how she hadn't detected him, but the blood magic stench gagged her now.

Through the bond, Roderick responded to her fear. First confusion, he didn't know what had terrified her. Then came the sense he was searching.

Alexander smirked at her, as he raised his voice and said, "What is she saying? What is Agnes saying?"

"She's beside herself with grief," the matron said. "Agnes doesn't know what she's saying."

"Yes, I do." Agnes flung herself away from the matron and staggered toward them. "My baby was sleeping, resting peacefully in her cradle. A little angel who sensed her mama was sick and didn't want to trouble her." Gaze darting from person to person, she jerked to a halt.

Waves of power emanated from Alexander, so strong Maeve could almost see them as vapor in the air. She retched and coughed as his magic crawled down her nose and throat.

Still more villagers drifted out of their cottages, clogging up the path between them and the church.

As Alexander stalked her, Maeve backed away.

"Good morning pretty cré-witch. Did you come to play?" he whispered.

"They thought I was too sick to know what they did." Spittle flew from Agnes's mouth. She lurched from one person to the next. "They took me for dead, or so near to it that it didn't signify. They took me for dead so they could steal the life from my baby."

"We came to help." Maeve had to raise her voice against the increasing babble. "We heard there was disease in the village, and we came to help." She waved her hand toward the cottages they had already visited. "Ask those who were sick, and they'll tell you. They'll tell you how they were sick and are now better."

"Better?" Malice gleamed in Alexander's dark eyes. His voice carried as he said, "You say better, I say bewitched."

Angry voices swirled around Maeve.

"What's Alexander saying?"

"Who killed Agnes's baby?" Prudence pushed to the front of the crowd. "What's happening here, Alexander?"

"I always said they were no good."

"My mum warned me to have nothing to do with them."

"You have bewitched them," Alexander said. The wave of power hit Maeve like a blow to her belly. Dark, metallic, rotten, the power that came of wresting magic through death, eddied and billowed around him like a dark cloak. "Your healing is nothing more than sorcery to turn them to your dark master."

Agnes screamed. "Satan! They are in league with Satan."

"Take them." Alexander grabbed her arm. "We must take them and force them to release our folk."

The matron tried to speak for them. "They're not—"

"They killed Agnes's baby." Prudence stood beside Alexander, her eyes glittering.

"They killed Agnes's baby so they could use her body for their black magic," Alexander said, and he should know. He was a creature of blood magic. Maeve hadn't even known that was possible. Her flesh shuddered where he touched.

"Well met, little Maeve," he whispered to her and smiled. "I want you to say my name in your mind. I want Roderick to know who killed you."

Roderick's fury lashed down their bond.

Voices roared in anger all about them. Disembodied accusations were thrust forward and grew wilder and wilder. The wall of bodies swelled and circled their small party.

Maeve had thought herself so clever in giving Roderick the slip. Now it rose to taunt her, and she screamed his name in her mind.

Alexander's grip on her arm tightened painfully. "That's

even better." His smile was more terrifying for its mesmerizing beauty. "Call him to you. Bring that whoreson to me."

She struggled against his hold, but he was strong, and the waves of blood magic buffeted her, draining her strength.

"They dance naked to entice men into their snare," Alexander yelled to the crowd. "Have congress with animals."

Maeve clawed at his hand, trying to make herself heard, to end this insanity. "None of that is true. We are servants of—"

"Satan. Servants of Satan," Alexander bellowed. "You heard her say it herself. She drinks the blood of newborns. Newborns like Agnes's baby."

The crowd grew around them in size and hysteria.

"They raise the dead." Alexander's grip bruised.

Agnes resumed her screaming. "My baby. They killed my baby and now they'll drink her blood."

"Check them for the mark, the mark of Satan," another man shouted.

Prudence's voice cut through the din. "We must subject them to the ordeal by water. It is the only way to know for sure."

"Aye." Alexander almost yanked her arm out of its socket. "The water trial. 'Tis the only sure way to know."

Sheila and her other healers huddled closer together. Pale as parchment, young Rose attempted to stay on her feet.

Maeve looked at her fellow blessed. They might die here today, and because of her. If she had listened to Roderick, none of them would be here. If she did nothing, Sheila and the others would die because of her.

"No," she shrieked, loud enough to scrape her throat raw. Loud enough for her voice to rise above the noise. "Not the water. Anything but the water."

Sheila stared at her in horror and shook her head.

"What are you up to?" Alexander hissed.

"I'll tell you anything you want to know." Maeve rolled her eyes about like a crazed person. Roderick was coming. All she had to do was distract the villagers until he got there. "I'll tell you all, only please, please don't put me in the water."

"See there." Prudence jabbed her finger in her face. "We have only to speak of the ordeal by water, and already she confesses."

"No." Sheila paled, shaking her head vehemently. "Don't do it."

"I'm a witch." Maeve cackled. "And Satan is my lover. I'm in league with the devil."

A woman screamed.

A man's voice rose in prayer.

Voices swelled about her, braying for blood. Her blood.

She pointed at the small cluster of healers. "I sucked the life out the baby. Not them. They're too stupid to know what to do."

Even above the noise of the villagers, she could hear Agnes wailing.

"They didn't do it." Maeve spat, narrowly missing the hem of Sheila's skirt. "They are weak. Mewling. He does not want them. He despises them."

"We must burn her," Prudence yelled in triumph. "It is the only way to be sure she's dead."

All this hated directed at her made Maeve feel ill. "You can't burn me," she screeched. "My dark lord will rise and pluck me from the fire."

Alexander's gaze stayed on her. "Give her to me, instead. I'll get the truth out of her."

The villagers had moved away from Sheila and the other healers. All attention was now on her.

"Yes," Prudence yelled. "Let Alexander have her. He knows what to do with these she-devils."

Agnes cackled. "Let Alexander have her."

She kept moving away. She didn't want to die. She had only recently celebrated her twenty-fifth year. She really, really didn't want to die. There was so much that she had yet to do, yet to discover.

The wall of bodies blocked her view of Sheila and the others. She willed them to run for safety. All eyes must stay on her. She raised her voice as loud as she could manage. "You can't kill me. The devil will save me."

Roderick's bloodthirsty bellow silenced the crowd. "Alexander."

As Alexander turned, his grip on her arm slackened. A feral smile twisted his face. "At last." He grinned and shoved Maeve at Agnes. "Hold her."

Sword raised, Roderick stalked through the crowd. "Let her go."

"I'm afraid not, Roderick." From beneath his doublet, Alexander pulled a sword. He swiveled his wrist, his sword catching the sunlight, as he waited for Roderick. "She knows too much, and my mother wants her dead."

Roderick reached Alexander and attacked. "Your mother must be used to disappointment by now."

12

Maeve stood stupefied as Roderick fought Alexander. Faster than her eye could follow, their steel flashed through the air. Blades met, clanged and struck sparks.

The watching villagers shrank back, giving them space.

Roderick and Alexander fixed hard stares on each other. The grim certainty of death as the only outcome shrouded both of them.

"Come on." Sheila pulled her arm.

Agnes lay crumpled behind her and Sheila still held the blood-stained log in both hands.

Maeve's brain was working too slowly. "You hit her."

"Aye, I bloody well hit her." Sheila growled. "Unnatural beast that she is. She used her baby's blood for the magic." She tugged on Maeve's arm. "Now come, while Roderick keeps them busy."

The crowd circled the fighting men. They were evenly matched but for Maeve there was only Roderick. "I need to help him."

"Don't be stupid." Sheila quickened her pace, dragging

Maeve behind her. "You're wasting the chance he's buying you. Now come."

Sheila was stronger than she looked, and Maeve couldn't break free. Trying to look behind her, she tripped over her feet. "He needs help."

"And he will get it," Sheila said. The other healers clustered around them as they ran for the churchyard. "But not from the likes of us. The other coimhdeacht will come for him."

A village woman glanced their way, froze, and turned back. "They're getting away," she screamed. "The witches are escaping."

More heads turned.

Steel clashed against steel and the villagers turned back to the fight.

"Go!" Sweat poured down Roderick's face. "Now, Maeve. Now."

"You must come." Sheila jerked her arm. "Don't render his sacrifice pointless."

Sacrifice. The word echoed through her entire being. Roderick had sacrificed himself for her. He'd tossed the dice on his own survival to ensure hers. It wasn't right. But Sheila wouldn't let go of her hand, and another healer had taken hold of her elbow and they tugged her between them.

Screams, grunts and shouts came from behind her. Yet, Maeve couldn't even turn to see how Roderick was faring. Inexorably she was compelled to keep running.

Even Rose managed to get her limp legs to move.

In the end, Maeve was half dragged, half pulled into the churchyard, down the narrow staircase to the crypt, and into the sudden quiet and dark below the church.

Only then did they stop, sides heaving as they tried to catch their breath.

"The incantation." Hands on her knees, Sheila bent over panting. "You're the only one who knows it."

Maeve stepped to the rock face and by rote uttered the words that would open the portal to safety. Her attention remained with Roderick in the village. Did he still live? She reached through their bond and felt him there. Please Goddess, let the strength with which being coimhdeacht imbued him save him now. As the other women stumbled into the passageway, Maeve stood to the side, her bond with Roderick as wide open as she could achieve without distracting him.

Three steps in, and the wards of Baile Castle encased the five healers. Maeve breathed a sigh of relief. Sheila and the other healers were now safe.

"Get back to the castle," she said. "Send the other coimhdeacht. Tell them Roderick needs them."

Sheila opened her mouth as if to argue, and then nodded. "You're going back for him."

"I can't abandon him. Especially not when it's my fault he's here." She motioned the healers to go. "There may be some small thing I can do to help him."

"Goddess bless you, Maeve."

"And you." Maeve whispered the incantation to Sheila. "Now get to safety."

Sheila closed the passage.

Maeve spun and ran back the way they had come. Twice, her rubbery legs brought her into painful and jarring contact with the ground. The noise from the village rolled on unabated. That had to be a good sign, right? It must be a sign Roderick was still fighting.

If the villagers caught sight of her, all would be lost. She had no intention of compounding her stupidity with yet more stupidity, so she kept herself hidden in the beech copse and crept closer to the heaving crowd.

She could start a fire, that would—

A victorious yell rose from the crowd, and several thrust their arms in the air.

Maeve's stomach churned, and her breath lodged like a barb her chest.

Sword raised for the killing blow, Alexander stood above Roderick.

Maeve pulled fire, her scream burning the back of her throat. Flame licked between her hands, wild and impatient, feeding off her churning emotions.

Yet, she couldn't do it. She couldn't send a fiery ball into the center of the people gathered about Roderick. It was her sacred oath as a cré-witch never to use her magic to harm. Even the trees about her were sacred.

Kneeling, Roderick fought. Sweat and blood streaming down his face, he brought his blade up in time to stop Alexander's. Blood soaked the white sleeve of his chemise and plastered it to his skin.

He lurched back to his feet.

The crowd pressed closer, now fearless in their much greater numbers and with Roderick showing signs of weakness.

Roderick crashed to his knees a second time. His head hung heavy on his neck, and his sword came up slower. He swayed and caught himself.

Gathering her strength, Maeve pushed it down the bond.

Up came Roderick's head.

The crowd bayed for blood. More of Roderick's precious blood, and he had already spilled too much.

"Goddess, help him," she whispered to the beech trees, standing in silent judgment all about her. "Goddess, please help him."

Roderick sagged. The bond went silent between them.

She pushed into the nothing, but he had blocked her as if he didn't exist.

A thick, black tendril shot from them Alexander to her. He spoke to Roderick, but Maeve could hear him as if he stood right beside her. "Be a brave boy, Roderick. Your witch is watching as I kill you." Alexander raised his sword. "Your death will stun her, and then she's mine."

Utter despair overpowered Roderick's block and almost brought Maeve to her knees. Roderick had failed her, and he knew it.

"Blessed." A hard hand shook her arm. "Get back to the keep."

Past her they streamed, intent and deadly, the other coimhdeacht. Swords, staffs, battle axes and daggers raised, they attacked the crowd surrounding Roderick.

Maeve barely dared hope they were real.

"Now." Thomas shook her arm again, his face an angry mask. "We need to get to Roderick, and we can't do so until you're safe."

Of course, it was their creed. To first save the blessed. Always blessed first. Whether she deserved such loyalty or not.

Maeve didn't even know all their names, these men who had come to save them. She should know the names of her saviors.

Thomas shook his head and shoved her in the direction of the church. "Go."

Her disobedience was the reason for this in the first place. Maeve stumbled, staggered and tripped her way toward the opening in the rock, and through it. Once on the safe side of the wards, she stopped.

She waited, her heart pounding loudly in her throat. Straining her ears, she tried to catch some hint of what was happening.

They appeared so suddenly they startled her. Bodies, big male bodies, crowded into the passageway and brushed past her. Someone muttered the incantation and the portal closed. Sweat and blood stink filled the narrow space. She was jostled out of the way and Maeve clung to the wall at her back.

The coimhdeacht were moving already, carrying someone between them.

"Roderick." She tried to peer through them to see if he still lived. Goddess please let him live. Hope clawed at her, painful in its uncertainty.

"Come." Thomas grabbed her arm and propelled her forward at a swift pace. "He breathes."

13

CRÉ·WITCH CHRONICLES

Maeve dipped her cloth in the basin of cool water and wiped Roderick's brow. He lay on his cot in the barracks. His fellow coimhdeacht moved around them. Not one word of condemnation had any of them spoken. Not even by a look had they blamed her for Roderick's condition. But Maeve knew it was all her fault. Roderick had told her, their bond worked better if there was honesty between them.

She hadn't listened and she deserved the censure of the coimhdeacht and also the combined condemnation of the entire coven. It wasn't her, however, who suffered most. If her punishment had affected her alone, she could have borne it much better. With fiendish accuracy Fiona had homed in on her weak spot and struck.

Because of her actions, six witches might have died, herself and the five healers. Compounding her disobedience was the charge that by using the secret passage to the church, she had risked someone in the village discovering it. Further, in order to save her, Roderick had risked his life. To her transgressions was added the risk to the other coimhdeacht who had rescued him.

Sickened by her own actions, Maeve had barely said a word during her disciplinary hearing with the council. What could she say? Her actions had been indefensible, and she was justly accused.

Her punishment, however, was unjust. No healer was permitted to attend Roderick during his convalescence. Maeve must nurse her coimhdeacht back to health alone. Only then, according to Fiona, would she truly understand the gravity of putting another's life at risk.

Maeve didn't agree. This punishment hurt Roderick more than it did her. Yet, he suffered it with inhuman stoicism. Maeve couldn't imagine how much pain he must be in but several of his ribs were broken, one of his legs, his face swollen until it was nigh unrecognizable, and the rest of him covered in deep purple welts and bruises. Alexander's blade had also found its mark across his thigh and shoulder and a vicious gash to his belly.

Yet, none of his pain or discomfort leaked into the bond. She wished it had, so she could at least feel what he felt.

As per Goddess's gift to all who protected her blessed, Roderick would heal completely and much faster than normal folk, but he wasn't immune to pain while his body knit back together.

As gently as she could, Maeve spread healing salve over Roderick's torso. Every one of his injuries silently rebuked her.

Slippers scraped softly over stone and Sheila joined her at Roderick's side. "How is he?"

"He doesn't complain."

Sheila shook her head. "I'll wager he doesn't."

She placed her healer's bag on the floor and opened it.

Maeve's mind slowed to a crawl. "What are you doing?"

"What does it look like?" Sheila snorted. "This man is in pain, and I'm a healer. I don't give a rat's arse what Fiona has to say on the matter. I also happen to owe this man my life."

"The council will be angry," Maeve said.

"Perhaps." Sheila shrugged. "But you were brave enough to risk their ire by taking us into the village in the first place, and I'm not so paltry as to stand back and allow both you and Roderick to suffer for fear of Fiona getting herself in a twist."

"Brave?" The word scalded the back of Maeve's throat. "What I did was stupid, not brave. As much as it galls me to admit this, Fiona is right about that. We all could have died."

Sheila shuddered. "And well I know it. But you didn't force us to go to the village."

"But my actions did force Roderick to come to my rescue." That fact remained inescapable. "His bond gives him no choice when I'm in danger."

"That much is true." Sheila nodded, rubbing her hands together. "But you don't bear the guilt of that alone, and we'll do what we can to ease his suffering. In this, my fellow healers and I are in perfect agreement."

Only part of that was true. The greater share of guilt remained firmly with her, but she wasn't going to argue the point and deprive Roderick of the help he needed. So, she shut her pie hole and let Sheila get to work.

"Absolutely savage," Sheila muttered, more to herself than anyone else. "To leave this man in so much pain. Unconscionable."

Maeve picked her words carefully. She'd had a lot of time to think and replay the scene in the village while she sat beside Roderick. Agnes's words replayed in her mind: *You shouldn't have interfered.* Agnes, and by extension Alexander and his mother, had known about her spirit walk with the original three. Other than Roderick, she had only told one other person about that. Perhaps Fiona had told Edana, or the rest of the council and the knowledge had leaked. Nothing stayed secret in the coven for long.

Maeve was in the unthinkable position of not knowing who

of her coven sisters she could trust. Not that many of them thought well of her right now. "Fiona seems to have considerable influence with the council."

"That's understating the matter." Sheila laid her palms on Roderick's chest. She closed her eyes and her breathing became deep and measured. Her body jerked rigid and her face contorted in pain.

Inside Roderick, Sheila's healing gift would hunt out the damage and reveal it to the healer. From there, the healer would act as a conduit, and pass the pain and injury through her body into the stones of Baile. When within the castle, the healer need not carry the injury. Here, Baile took it from her directly and fed it into the earth.

"There." Sheila stepped back, considerably paler now than when she'd entered the room. Healing was a selfless gift, in which the healers never hesitated to place themselves in the path of injury and disease. "That's the worst of it. The rest his body will take care of swiftly enough."

"How is Rose?" Maeve hadn't seen the youngest healer since they'd returned to Baile. Not that she'd seen many people, with most of the castle united in their condemnation of her.

Sheila's face grew pinched, and she shook her head. "She isn't recovering as quickly as we would like." She glanced at Maeve and growled. "Now don't go laying that on your shoulders as well. We had no business taking such an inexperienced witch to the village, and well we knew it."

Sheila put a vial of pale-yellow liquid on the table beside Roderick's bed. "If he wakes and looks to be in discomfort, give him a few drops of that." She fastened the straps on her healer's bag. "No, we made the decision to take Rose with us. She has kin in the village, and she was worried about them. But she's young to her power, and that contagion was stronger than we supposed."

"She'll be alright though?" The healers always recovered faster than anyone else.

"We'll keep an eye on her," Sheila said and picked up her bag. "There is more in that village to worry us than the contagion." She shuddered and looked ill. "But for now, you concern yourself with the big fellow here, and we'll worry about Rose."

After Sheila left, Maeve drew a chair up to Roderick's bedside and sat.

He breathed easier since Sheila's visit, taking in fuller, deeper drafts of air. His face was also more relaxed. Even in deep sleep, Roderick looked fierce, the lines of his face too uncompromising to ever claim boyishness. With his fighter's grace and powerful form, he was the sort of man who made girls giggle and try to catch his eye. He deserved a better witch, one more cognizant of the honor bestowed on her by Goddess in granting her a coimhdeacht in the first place.

However, she could and would do better, and he would recover much faster now that Sheila had visited.

Some of the tension in Maeve's chest eased. Still, Sheila hadn't assured her Rose would be fine and Maeve would only truly rest easy when the young healer was declared out of harm's way.

Roderick's dry rasp made her jump. "You're frowning."

"How are you feeling?" She scrambled to her feet, feeling better when she was standing.

Roderick grimaced. "I'll live. I've had worse."

She nodded. Not knowing what to do with her hands, she clasped them in front of her. The silence vibrated with all the things she wanted to say but couldn't bring herself to say. Mostly she wanted to embrace him and tell him how relieved she was that he was still alive and on his way to recovery.

She shouldn't be standing there with a mouthful of teeth, clueless as to what to say next. The bond between blessed and coimhdeacht was unbreakable, for life. They needed to do better than this constant sniping and bickering. She needed to do better.

Maeve took her seat. She leaned forward and gave his hand a quick pat. "I'm glad you're going to be all right."

"Really?" He looked at her and smirked.

"I'm sorry. I'm so, so sorry. More sorry than I can say." The words rushed out her mouth.

Roderick stared at her.

Having come this far, she may as well finish the matter. "I'm sorry for causing all of this. I should have listened to you and never gone to the village.

Frowning, Roderick peered at her face. "Are you feeling guilty? About what happened?" He waved a hand down his length. "About what happened to me?"

"Yes." That hardly needed clarification, but she was truly remorseful, and being sharp with him would undermine that.

"Maeve." Roderick chuckled and shook his head. "I appreciate the apology, I really do. But I have been coimhdeacht for over five hundred years, and before that I was a knight. This is hardly the first fight I've lost, and sadly it won't be the last." He held up his hand to silence her when she would speak. "You're the third witch I've served as guardian."

"I know about Tahra, but not much about Brigid," she said, still not sure he would even welcome a closer connection between them.

He nodded. "Brigid was older when I was assigned to her, and she had a specific task to accomplish. She chose to move on once it was completed."

"And then me?" She was too remorseful to press for details.

Roderick nodded. "And then you. I'm well acquainted with the nature of cré-witches. I was angered when I discovered you'd gone anyway, but hardly surprised."

"Oh." All in all, she felt rather deflated. Her major transgression seemed to amount to more or less what he expected of her. "Well, still, I'm sorry. And I hated seeing you get hurt."

"I accept your apology," he said, "and no more enjoyed getting hurt than you enjoyed watching it."

Guilt washed over her anew.

"Maeve," he growled in that officious manner of his. "Stop looking so stricken. I'll be fine, and you'll be back to calling me names beneath your breath in no time."

Heat climbed her cheeks. She'd do well to remember his excellent hearing in the future.

"Of a more pressing concern," he said, shifting in his bed, "is that it looks like Rhiannon has friends within Baile."

14

M aeve was glad Roderick couldn't leave his bed to see this. She stayed on the battlements long past when the other witches left and stared at the gibbet. Two more bodies had joined Jane, Rebecca and Molly. Two women who had raised their voices in her defense and now swung lifelessly beside the others.

Her face blackened and bloodied, the matron who had first challenged Agnes hung beside a younger woman.

Pinned to the top of the gibbet, a rough wooden sign stated in hasty rust-colored letters: Witches Must Die.

Edana joined her at the parapet and leaned forward between the crenellations.

Maeve tensed, sure that whatever Edana had to say, she didn't want to hear.

"Come to view your handiwork?" Edana sneered. "He deserves so much better than you."

Possibly for the first time in their lives, she agreed with Edana. Roderick did deserve better. Better than her, for certain, but also better than a merciless bitch who used the death of innocent women to score a blow against a coven sister.

With Tahra, Roderick had experienced better, but for now he was stuck with her. Neither of them had chosen their bond, and for all her resistance, it was now Roderick who paid the price. "You're right," she said. "But until Goddess herself breaks this bond, I'm all he has."

She turned and walked away. Two younger witches scowled at her as she passed. Maeve wished she could say she grew immune to the hostility, but each glare scraped her raw.

Taking the back way to the barracks, via the training yards, she slipped into the main area where a few coimhdeacht lounged at tables. A small group by the window were playing dice. They glanced up when she entered, nodded, and went back to their game.

Through a rough arch, she entered the training area. Steel clanged as two men sparred. She skirted the sandy area and entered the sleeping rooms.

Thomas stepped out of the bathing area. A drying cloth rode the slim jut of his hips. Above the white cloth, water clung to the battle hewn lines of his chest.

A small smile tilting his mouth, Thomas sauntered toward her and stopped right in front of her. "Blessed."

"Thomas." Her throat dried and heat thrummed beneath her skin. She must be all shades of red if the warmth flooding her face was any indication.

Crowding even closer, until she could smell his clean skin and soap combination, Thomas tilted her chin up. His beautiful hazel eyes studied her. "Still persecuting yourself, I see?"

"No."

He raised an eyebrow, calling her a liar.

The burden of guilt pressed down on her. "He was hurt, almost killed, because of me."

"Maeve," Thomas purred. "Roderick is hurt because it's the nature of who he is. It's the risk we all accept." His gaze caressed her face and down over her breasts. "And for the most part, it's a risk well worth taking."

"Thomas, are you flirting with me?" She couldn't be sure. The experience was that new to her.

White teeth flashing as he laughed, Thomas shook his head. "Clearly, I'm losing my touch."

Maeve wouldn't go that far. For the first time in days she felt like smiling.

"Thomas," Roderick barked from behind Thomas.

Still grinning, Thomas turned and faced Roderick.

Roderick approached them, wearing his breeches and several bandages. He also wore the most ferocious frown Maeve had yet to see. Fortunately, he kept most of it reserved for Thomas. "Have you nothing better to do?"

"Not really." Thomas winked at Maeve. "Not with you laid up."

A muscle ticked in Roderick's jaw, and his scowl deepened. "I'm back on my feet now."

"How fortunate," Thomas drawled and gave Maeve a melting smile. "We hardly knew how to entertain ourselves without you."

Smirk still in place, he brushed past Maeve and whispered in her ear, "And yes, I was flirting. Think about it."

Roderick stood there and glowered.

While he did, she took a moment to compare a near naked Roderick to a near naked Thomas.

And thank you, Goddess, for showering your bounty on this worthless witch.

"Are you feeling better?" Roderick was broader than Thomas but an inch or so shorter. Thomas resembled a wolf: rangy, strong and graceful. Roderick was all prime bull. The thought made her snort with laughter.

Roderick's cold gaze snapped back to her. "Watch out for Thomas. He likes a new conquest in his sheets."

"It would be an improvement to being drowned while still a virgin." She had spoken before she could censor her thought.

Roderick's eyes widened.

Even knowing it was a lost cause, she clapped her hands over her mouth.

"Maeve." Roderick's expression changed. Intent and slumberous, he gazed down at her. "There are better men to help you with that."

"Like who?" She glanced about them.

Roderick grasped her elbow and walked her back to his chamber. "Where have you been? And Thomas is right, you look like a whipped dog."

"Thomas never said that." She nearly tripped over her feet. "Could we go back to the last thing."

He frowned. "The whipped dog?"

"Before that." Maeve dug her heels in and forced him to stop.

Flashing her a grin at least as wicked as Thomas's, Roderick stopped. "You mean the part about other men?"

Her face nearly exploded with heat. "Yes, that part."

"Don't look so shocked, Maeve." Roderick touched her cheek. "You're lovely and Thomas isn't the only one to notice." He got them moving again. "Now tell me what has got under your skin?"

"I was on the parapet, and Edana joined me there." Guilt returned and chased other thoughts away. "Two more villagers have been hanged."

"That's unfortunate." Roderick scowled. "I'm sure Edana used their deaths to heap the blame on you."

"It's no more than I deserve."

"Maeve." Roderick stopped and gripped her shoulders. "None of this is your fault."

She gazed at the bandages still strapped over his middle. "I'm certain that it is."

"The dissention in the village had been brewing for a while." Roderick slid his arm around her shoulders. "And now we know who is behind it."

Maeve allowed herself to be enfolded in his warmth. Her cheek pressed to the smooth skin of his chest, his waist trim and strong as she slid her arms about him. He was her coimhdeacht; she was allowed to draw comfort from him. She wouldn't be the first witch to do so. And more.

"But I have more bad news." His voice rumbled beneath her ear. "Sheila was just with me."

Maeve's belly dropped. She read the answer through their bond.

"The young healer. Rose?" Roderick's big hand spanned her back. "She has contracted the village contagion."

Maeve reeled. Even as the logical part of her brain rejected the accusation, guilt wriggled round to the side door and let himself in. Determined to prove to all those misguided enough to side with Fiona and the council that she knew better, she'd allowed pride to lead them here.

"That's not your fault either." Roderick leaned closer to her and spoke beside her ear.

"Rose is ill," she said. "She's infected with whatever ails the village."

"And the healers chose to take her. She wanted to help because she had family in the village." Roderick hissed a breath and eased back from her.

"You should be in bed." She needn't have bothered, as Roderick would only do as he deemed necessary.

"And you should stop taking responsibility for that which isn't yours to shoulder." Roderick shifted his weight and eased closer to her. "Let me guess what you're thinking."

Maeve shrugged. What a pity it had taken this to have her and Roderick groping their way toward functioning as a pair.

He took her shrug as permission and folded his arms.

"You're thinking that if not for you and your stubborn insistence on showing the healers the way to the village, I wouldn't have been hurt, and the others wouldn't have been exposed to the danger." He sniffed. "And in this you're right."

"Thanks." She hastily stamped on the hurt. She much preferred Thomas's version of comfort.

"I speak only the truth." He shrugged. "I'll never lie to you, Blessed. Of this you can be sure. Sometimes the truth I offer won't be welcome, but it'll always be the truth as I see it." He took her hand. "I tell you this, so you'll know you may always trust my word. I'll never soften the truth to spare your feelings, nor will I allow you to shoulder what isn't yours to bear."

Maeve stared at where her hand was engulfed by his much larger one. "I should have listened to you."

"Maybe." He squeezed her hand. "But you acted with your conscience, and for that I can't fault you. You believed the villagers needed the healers, and it was the healers who made the decision to go. You merely provided the path. They chose to set their feet upon it. Look at me."

He waited until she dragged her gaze up to his.

The cold blue of his eyes warmed. "And now Edana comes and whispers her poison in your ear. I've seen fighting men like her. Their gift is in understanding their opponent's weakness and homing in on it with unerring skill. But as skilled as she is at it, you're the one who allows her into your mind. It's you who gives her poison a home." He turned then and limped away from her.

"Roderick." She followed him. "Do you think I did the right thing?"

He growled at her over his shoulder. "Again, Blessed, you're short of hearing. It matters not whether I think you did the right thing. It matters only whether you think you did."

"I don't know."

"Then ask yourself this," he said. "If knowing what you know now, you were presented with the same choice, do you still believe you did the right thing in taking the healers to the village?"

15

Yes. The answer to Roderick's question was yes. Even
had she known beforehand the uncomfortable conse-
quences now hers to bear, she still would have acted
as she had.

They were cré-witches, tasked by Goddess to serve human-
ity. Their extraordinary gifts were given not so they could hide
in Baile Castle assured of their safety. Their gifts had been
given to spare Goddess's creation from suffering.

So, yes, even knowing all she did now, she would still have
taken the healers to the village. A certainty that became more
sorely tested as the days wore on and more young witches fell
to the plague.

The acolytes and the apprentices, and even the journeywomen, were as susceptible to the disease as the villagers. Even
with their connection to Goddess, and repeated wielding of
magic for protection, as the days wore on, the older witches
fell too.

A dark column of smoke hung constantly over the village,
carrying with it the stench of burning flesh. The sick within
Baile had the full strength of the healers. The villagers had only

the small medical knowledge their wise women possessed, most of that gleaned from the healers in the first place.

Five days after their ill-fated trip to the village, Maeve woke in the middle of the night to her chamber full of images from Rose's life. The summoning familiar, but no less tragic, was Rose's spirit calling out to her to scribe Rose's story on the cavern walls so her mortal body could pass.

Maeve understood death so much more than the average person. But Rose had been so young, and so full of promise and the mortal part of Maeve cried for the loss of such a beautiful, light-filled girl. She dressed, not hurrying but neither did she tarry. Rose's soul would wait for her.

She lit a lamp and let herself into the dark, silent corridor.

A large form materialized from the dark. Roderick.

Maeve had journeyed to a deathbed many times, but always on her own. She jumped a bit when Roderick's large hand folded around hers, offering her silent comfort. She took the comfort he offered.

They reached the healer's hall and Maeve let her gift guide her.

Two mature healers kept vigil by Rose's bed. One of them was Sheila and she was bent over Rose, her hands on the younger woman, trying to draw the illness out of her.

It was too late.

She looked up and saw Maeve and paled. "No." She sobbed and shook her head. "Please, no."

The other healer, a tiny, brunette clapped both hands over her mouth and stared at Maeve. Huge brown eyes filled with tears. "Please," she whispered. "Give us more time. If we had more time."

Maeve hated this part of her gift. It felt more like a curse. Mourners begged her for more time, as if she had any control. No, the spirits came to her, tired of fighting, weary of pain, depleted by this life and ready to pass beyond.

So, Maeve said what she always did, "Rose feels no pain now. She's ready to go."

"Goddess, no." Tears streamed down Sheila's face. "She's not yet twenty. So young. So gifted. This can't be right."

Maeve approached the bed slowly. Once she took Rose's soul, the body would die. Rose's story would flow from her onto the walls of the caverns as sigils. Rose would never be forgotten, nor the story of her journey as a cré-witch.

Rose's spirit hovered near her body. Sometimes the spirits wanted her to say something to the bystanders. Others were confused, not sure of what happened next. Rose's spirit flared a brilliant pearlescent white, as beautiful in its essence as the girl had been in life, already no longer tied to this realm and needing only Maeve to guide it to the next.

"Come." She spoke aloud for the benefit of the living. The spirit had already responded to her beckoning. As always, the spirit entering Maeve was like frigid water filling her skin to capacity. Rose's memories played through her mind. Her life experience, everything Rose had learned or knew, said and done, seen, sensed, smelled, touched, heard and tasted all shared space within Maeve.

"No." Sheila wailed as the breath left Rose's body. She gathered the girl's body and rocked it.

Maeve could tell her that Rose was already gone, but the grief belonged to the living. Mourning was as much a part of being alive as death.

Maeve trudged back through the empty castle, Roderick by her side.

A stiff wind buffeted them as they crossed the bailey to the door in the wall. Beyond the door, on the seaward side, the wind enthusiastically tugged at her hair and clothes. Fine ocean spray dampened her skin and turned her lips salty.

In the caverns the dead waited to receive one of theirs.

As Maeve crossed the threshold, all the crystals glowed. A

thousand soft chimes filled the air, strangely discordant and harmonious at once.

Roderick drew a harsh breath but stayed beside her as they moved from cavern to cavern until they found the space Rose's spirit guided her to.

After fetching her basket, Maeve lit her brazier and surrendered self to Rose. From the basket, she took the shells and crystals, knowing her blessing would guide them into the pattern representing the soul of a being who had, in this incarnation, been born woman, who had walked amongst the créwitches as one of them, learned to be a healer and been named Rose. Under Maeve's guiding hands the pattern formed and sunk into the rock.

Rose's spirit flowed from her into the pattern on the wall in a heady rush of senses, emotions, and memories. And then Rose was gone.

Maeve slumped, suddenly exhausted, and her own grief, held at bay while she did what she was called by Goddess to do, burst from her and Maeve sobbed.

In the past she had lain, alone and exhausted, and sobbed into the cold cavern rock. This time, Roderick picked her up, like she weighed no more than a small child and held her. "There now," he murmured against her hair as he carried her from the caverns. "You did well."

"But this is only the beginning."

A BELL TOLLED from deep within the keep and woke Maeve. By the angle of sun on her chamber floor, it was late afternoon. The bell meant all the witches were being called to a meeting.

Maeve hurried and finished dressing. She opened her chamber door to Roderick leaning against the far wall. "You'll come with me?"

He nodded and relief flooded her. Rose's death would touch the entire coven.

Mostly silent, witches filed into the great hall. Some still wept, whilst others showed signs of having recently dried their tears. Still others huddled in small groups and spoke softly amongst themselves.

Maeve took a seat near the healers.

Face drawn and haggard, Sheila stood and hugged her. She took Maeve's hand and pulled her down on the bench to sit beside her.

Maeve clung to her a moment.

On the dais, the council stood around Fiona.

"That bodes ill." Roderick's deep voice was for her ears only.

Edana looked up suddenly and caught her eye. The look of cold triumph in Edana's gaze chilled Maeve to the bone.

Roderick touched her shoulder, a quiet reminder that he was there, and he stood with her.

From amongst her fellow healers, and not from amongst the council where her position as head healer should have placed her, Joy stood.

Slowly at first, as if people were reluctant to acknowledge Joy and the news she bore, a charged silence filled the hall.

Joy waited for absolute quiet before she spoke. "I'm here to share the death of one of our journeywomen." She clasped her hands before her so tightly her knuckles turned white. "Despite our best efforts, we were unable to save Rose."

About her, Maeve sensed the healers' grief. The idea of losing one of their own throbbed like a neglected wound. Around the hall, other witches also drew close to their own, seeking comfort and affirmation of life.

"We ask that you mourn with us." Joy's voice cut like jagged glass through the hall. "We ask that you join with us in mourning a sister taken well before her time. We commend

Rose to Goddess and return our sister to her infinite care. Blessed be."

"Blessed be," murmured the hall.

Maeve tried to draw comfort from those two words, which she uttered daily without thinking what they truly meant. They were a recognition of their service to Goddess. More importantly they were an affirmation of the bond between Goddess and blessed. An acknowledgment that in this, like in everything else, Goddess watched over them, guided them, and protected them.

But the peace that usually accompanied those words escaped her.

Goddess had raised Rose to be beside her. Her trust must always be in Goddess, whom she served. Some days however, and this day was one of them, trust came hard.

"With respect." Fiona held up her hand. "There is more at play here than the death of one witch."

An uneasy ripple ran through the hall, and Joy tensed. "Now isn't the time."

"Your pain touches all of us." Fiona clasped her hands before her chest. A dark smudge appeared behind Fiona and disappeared.

It was gone so fast Maeve couldn't even be sure she'd seen anything. She glanced over her shoulder to Roderick.

Like a wolf arrowing in on his prey, he studied Fiona intently. Fiona's continued silence about the lost one and blood magic in the village chafed him as much as it did her. Events within and around Baile were gaining dizzying momentum and Fiona didn't appear to be doing anything about it.

"One of our sisters has died today," Fiona said. "And as much as I wish it so, I can't say blessed be."

Shock reflected in the faces all around her.

"I can't say blessed be"—Fiona raised her voice—"because in my heart I don't believe this death came from Goddess."

Joy sprang to her feet. "What are you saying?"

"I'm saying that Rose was indeed taken from us." Fiona paused to wipe tears from her cheeks. "But my heart is sore because it's not Goddess who took Rose from us, but one of our own." Silence fell about the hall, and Fiona looked directly at Maeve.

Gazes followed Fiona's and landed on her. Most looked genuinely confused, but some stares held sharp condemnation. They blamed her for Rose's death.

Shock held Maeve immobile.

A warning rumble came from Roderick, and he moved close enough for her to feel the heat emanating from him.

"How dare you." Joy's plump form shook with outrage. "How dare you use this death in such a way."

"Me?" Fiona looked aghast. "I'm not the one whose ill-conceived decision led to the death of a young witch."

Around Joy, healers sprung to their feet, each one shouting louder than the other.

Roderick slid his hand beneath her elbow and tugged her to her feet. He tucked her on his left side and drew his sword with his right. His message resonated on the shocked faces staring at them.

Fiona gaped at him. "Coimhdeacht! You serve this coven and Goddess."

"I serve this witch." Roderick put himself between her and the hall. Behind him, his fellow coimhdeacht gathered in support. "And until Goddess herself tells me I don't, my life for Maeve's."

"It's lore." Thomas stood beside Roderick. "A coimhdeacht serves his witch, forsaking all others. It's who we are and what we stand for and by."

"They're right." Lavina shot to her feet. "The bond between witch and coimhdeacht is inviolate. It predates the council even."

Mutters and murmurs followed her pronouncement.

Edana stood and raised her voice to be heard over the babble. "Don't be distracted from the issue at hand." She pointed at Maeve. "Because of her, a young witch is dead."

It hit Maeve like a punch.

Thomas gave her a glance loaded with sympathy and shook his head. He didn't blame her.

Roderick's attention remained on the hall. Tension radiated from him to her.

"Fiendishly clever." Thomas grunted and shook his head.

Stung, Maeve turned to confront him. "You believe her?"

Unabashed, Thomas waved her to silence. "You miss the point." He indicated the hall around them. "Look."

Coven sister faced off with coven sister, the anger between them palpable. Voices raised and raised higher as witches stopped listening to each other.

"They're all fighting," she said.

"Exactly." Roderick nodded. "But look who's not fighting."

Across the hall, Fiona sat, a smug smile on her face.

"Come." Roderick touched her arm. "She doesn't know yet that you've seen through her, and it would be best if we kept it that way."

"But why?" In the safety of her own bedchamber, Maeve gave vent to her feelings.

Roderick checked the corridor before shutting the door and bolting it. "Fiona ferments dissent and we both saw who she serves."

"We can't be right about this." Unable to sit still, Maeve paced.

Roderick positioned himself by the door. "You saw the same thing I saw. In the hall. Remember what I said about her before? She already knew about Rhiannon before you told her about what the first had said."

Maeve shivered and wrapped her arms about her. "And she asked us not to tell anyone. Like she was concealing it from the rest of the coven."

"The evidence mounts." Roderick shrugged. "In the village, Alexander made you his target."

Maeve couldn't entertain what Roderick suggested. "That was because of you."

"Partly." Roderick paced. "That whoreson would do anything to get at me, but he was prepared to let the other five go to ensure he got you."

"You're suggesting he wanted me dead?" Maeve hated that Roderick made so much sense.

He nodded and kept pacing. "And the one thing you did out of the ordinary—"

"Besides bonding you?"

"I bonded you." A smile ghosted over his face. "You went to Fiona with your suspicions. And now, this night, she tried to unite the entire hall against you."

"She did more than try." Most of the faces turned her way tonight had done so in condemnation. "She has turned most of them against me, and now anything I say about the lost one and what I know looks like a weak attempt to justify my actions."

16

CRÉ-WITCH CHRONICLES

F our days later, along with her coven sisters, Maeve kept a grim, silent vigil on the battlements as a growing knot of villagers loomed at the outer edge of the wards, watching and waiting, looking for a way in to Baile Castle.

Too few witches stood on the battlements as the contagion swept through the castle. All night Maeve had led spirits to beyond and scribed their stories on the cavern walls.

The sight of Alexander stepping forward hardly came as a surprise. "We'll burn you devil bitches out of the there."

"Oh, dear." An apprentice paled and swayed beside her. "Can they get in?"

"No." Maeve put as much certainty as she could muster into her reply. The wardens had assured the coven the wards would hold. That wasn't what concerned Maeve most. Waves of malevolence crept from the villagers. Blood magic prickled through the air, like steel filings against her skin. She couldn't say how many of her coven sisters recognized the taste/scent signature of blood magic.

"I'll make that whoreson eat his steel." Roderick locked his gaze on Alexander. "We kill him, and the rest will scatter like mice."

Yesterday there had been barely a handful. Today the number had swelled to over thirty, including many familiar faces who had turned to the cré-witches for help a time or two. Agnes came to the forefront of the group. "My baby," she screamed. "Give me back the soul of my wee, dead girl."

A roar rose from the villagers.

Roderick murmured for her ear only. "If Alexander is here, Rhiannon won't be far behind. She won't risk him being alone this close to Baile."

"Can you see...her?" Maeve dared not say her name aloud.

Roderick squinted against the muted sun and searched the crowd. "You don't know what she looks like?"

"No." Maeve kept her eyes on Alexander. Goosebumps prickled her skin. Alexander was looking right at her and Roderick. "When I spirit walk, she's only there as a shadow. Not even an image of her lingers in the firsts' memories."

Roderick grunted, all his attention on the distant figure of Alexander. His fingers curled around his sword pommel. "When they severed her connection to Goddess, they must have severed her connection to all witches."

"We're surrounded." Maeve shifted closer to the stalwart Roderick. "If they get through the gates—"

"I'll be here." Roderick touched the small of her back.

Maeve held back a sigh. "Almost hourly. It grows."

"They've called for Matthew Hopkins," Roderick said. "They've invited him here to officiate over your trials once they break through the wards."

"How can they be so certain they will break through?" At the fore of the villagers, a lanky man faced the castle. He raised his fist and shook it in their direction.

"That's what bothers me." Roderick pushed his hand

through his hair. "It is as if they wait for something or someone."

Maeve nodded. "Could she do it? Does she have that sort of power?"

"I wouldn't have thought so." Roderick shook his head. "When we severed her connection, we believed we had destroyed her access to magic. Nobody anticipated her gaining control over blood magic. It's powerful, unpredictable, and it would take a witch of enormous power to master it."

Rhiannon had been the most powerful of the first, and now she was as ancient as the ground beneath their feet. There was no predicting how much power she could wield.

Maeve recoiled instinctively from the idea. "How does she access the blood magic?"

"An excellent question, and one we need to save for when the village isn't trying to overrun the castle." Roderick's face settled into grim lines. "We achieve nothing by speculating, other than making ourselves nervous."

"I didn't think you got nervous." Maeve glanced at him.

Roderick suppressed a smile but not fast enough that Maeve didn't catch a glimmer of it. "I don't," he said. "I was referring to your nerves."

Cold slithered over her skin and raised the hair on her nape.

Roderick stilled. His gaze snapped to the gate.

"What is it? Maeve followed his stare, rubbing her arms to alleviate the odd sensation, like a toothache over her entire body.

"The wards." He unsheathed his sword as he ran for the entrance. "The wards have failed."

Maeve stared at his retreating back. The wards didn't fail. They couldn't fail. It was impossible.

Shock broadsided her coven sisters. Some whimpered,

others went silent, still others whispered amongst themselves, their fear palpable.

While they stood frozen, angry villagers poured over the drawbridge.

From the gatehouse, the coimhdeacht moved to intercept them, Roderick at their head.

Calm, disciplined, and deadly, they moved as if they shared one mind. Weapons wielded with awful precision, they met the onslaught on the drawbridge and drove them back.

The angry rabble was too disorganized to mount much of a defense against the implacable force facing them, and they fell back.

Roderick's sword flashed in the meager sunlight, rising and falling as he and his men drove the attackers from the draw-bridge, and over the stone bridge spanning the deep gully between the village and the castle.

Maeve couldn't take her eyes off him. Their bonding was a mixed blessing.

Steadily, the coimhdeacht drove the villagers back. The invaders stopped where the castle wards should have been, Baile's only line of defense.

Watching Roderick fight provided a kind of torment she hoped never to live again. Even knowing how skilled he was, her foolish fears wouldn't be comforted. She wouldn't breathe freely again until he was back safely behind the wards.

She stood on the battlements amongst her coven sisters and no one spoke to her, or even acknowledged her. Her isolation from her coven sisters stung now more than ever. She would dearly have loved to watch the fighting with other sisters bonded to coimhdeacht, share their mutual fears and perhaps even draw comfort from the older sisters who knew better. But they were down in the barracks, and Fiona had made her a pariah with the other witches.

She stared until her eyes watered. Her gaze fixed on

Roderick as if she could somehow will him to be safe. Until he had rescued her in the village, she had never considered that something other than her choosing to journey beyond would sever their bond. She refused to accept that having survived the villagers to save her, Roderick would die at their hands anyway. Yet, he had so recently been injured. Pray Goddess his strength was where it should be.

Like the ancient stones of the castle itself, Roderick had always been there. Baile Castle without him, and now her life without him, was unthinkable. She yanked her thoughts away from that direction, which was singularly unhelpful to either her or Roderick.

Magic surged and crackled through the castle, raising the hair on her nape and rubbing across her skin. Warden magic. Maeve hardly dared breathe. Her gaze remained fixed on the men at the gates, they would sense the moment the wards came back into place.

Roderick dropped his sword first, and then nodded to the others. One by one, the coimhdeacht lowered their weapons.

A burly man standing near the front of the villagers gave a yell and lunged. He hit the wards and was repelled six feet back in the road.

Maeve took the first full breath she'd taken since Roderick had left her in the caverns.

The coimhdeacht pulled back to the gatehouse, where they left two men to stand guard. The remainder returned to the castle.

Maeve shoved past the knot of sisters and clattered down the stairs. Outside the great hall, coven sisters congested the hallway and Maeve used her elbows to great effect.

"Oy!" Madalyn, a friend of Edana's, yelled and grabbed for her.

"Bide," another witch said. "She goes to see how her coimhdeacht fares."

She ran through the hall. The corridor leading to the barracks was quiet and she ran faster.

Several bonded witches milled about the barracks when she reached them. They nodded to her and made a space amongst them. From what Maeve had seen, none of the coimhdeacht had been harmed in the fighting, or even come close to getting hurt, but that didn't matter to the women in the room. Like a flock of broody hens, they needed to make sure their chicks were safe.

Chicks in this instance referred to a group of overly large, heavily armed and deadly fighters. Maeve snorted back a giggle. An older sister looked at her and grinned, as if she understood what Maeve was thinking.

The door opened and the men filed in.

Sweat and blood streaking his handsome face, Thomas strolled through. He winked at her and went to join Lavina. They embraced and Lavina stared into his face as if to assure herself he really was hale. Thomas gave Lavina a genuine and tender smile before drawing her into a hug.

Scenes of joyful reunion happened all around Maeve. Some witches contented themselves with a more sedate embrace, but others threw themselves bodily at their guardians.

Roderick entered last, his huge shoulders filling the doorway.

Shyness beset Maeve, and she had no idea what to do next.

Roderick glanced at a couple to his right. The pair was engaged in a particularly fervent kiss. He looked back to her, grimaced and raised one eyebrow.

Maeve giggled, and her shyness melted away. She approached Roderick and stopped a foot in front of him. "You're well?"

He nodded and touched a finger to her cheek. "I'm well."

Maeve stayed with him as he went to the hall to get something to eat. He had taken a few moments to wash the evidence of his fighting away, and like many of her bonded coven sisters, Maeve had stayed in the barracks and waited for him to do so. He returned from the kitchen with an impressively loaded plate and sat beside her.

Clearly, fighting was hungry work. She poured him a goblet of wine and gave it to him.

He raised that supercilious brow at her. "I'm touched."

"Just drink it." Maeve's cheeks heated. Tomorrow she intended to go back to carping at him, but for now she felt too much relief for that. "Thank goodness the wards are back up."

"Indeed." Roderick wasted no time in spooning stew into his mouth. "But they won't hold."

Maeve stared at him. He chewed and swallowed as she waited for him to explain.

"The fix is temporary." He pulled apart a loaf of bread and dunked a piece into his bowl. "I have a sense of Baile." He touched his free fist to his chest. "In here. All the coimhdeacht do, but mine is stronger than the others." He shrugged. "Maybe because I built her, or maybe because I'm older than the rest, but I can sense her and how she fares."

Roderick's bone, blood and skin were melded into the stones of Baile.

"The wards—" He shook his head and tore another piece from the loaf. "They will withstand the villagers, but not whoever, or whatever brought them down in the first place."

The repercussions of what Roderick said were enormous. Maeve took a piece of his bread and chewed. She swallowed without tasting it.

If magic had brought the wards down, someone within Baile had helped bring them down, a warden witch, and one of power and in a position of trust.

17

Maeve shivered, the grass freezing beneath her feet. A charcoal sky stretched from horizon to horizon, jagged bolts of red lightning tearing through it. Trees loomed dark and forbidding above the forest clearing, their limbs, bare of leaves and ghostly, stretching toward her.

"Only one can live." Tahra emerged from the mist shrouding the forest. Her red dress garish against the frosted ground, she stayed far back. "You must remain stalwart, Maeve. We are depending on you to bear the impossible burden." The figure flickered. "We must do what we can, or all is lost. All of us must do all we can."

"Maeve!" Roderick wasn't part of her dream. He shook her shoulder hard enough to yank her back to her cold bedchamber.

Hanging over her, his face was drawn into tight tense lines. "Get up." He dropped her cloak onto the bed beside her. Her sturdy walking boots followed. "I've got to get you to the caverns."

Maeve stared at her boots her tired mind struggling to catch up. The air around them crackled with live magic, witches casting faster than she could follow. "What's happening?"

"Maeve," Roderick said forcefully enough to drag her attention away from the rapidly escalating magic all about them. "If you regret doubting me before, you'll come with me now without arguing." He shook her cloak at her. "I have a few minutes to get you to the caverns and they're ticking away rapidly."

Maeve jumped out of bed and pulled her cloak around her. The chill of the flagstones stung the bottom of her feet and she hauled on her walking boots. "Let's go."

Roderick took her arm in a firm grip and opened the door to the corridor. A scream echoed down the hallway and Roderick yanked her back in time to avoid a collision with a witch running full tilt away from them.

Patricia, one of Fiona's, ran past them without a glance, her face hard with determination.

"The wards are down." Roderick pulled her into the corridor and hustled her along it. "They're all the way down this time, and Fiona isn't letting anybody reset them."

She had so many questions, but Roderick took the stairs two at a time and forced her to pay attention or risk breaking her neck.

"You." A tall witch stepped into her path and scowled at Maeve. Around her the air sparked as she reached for her magic.

Maeve stared at her dumbfounded. Her befuddled brain couldn't even put a name to her coven sister. A coven sister who reached for her magic to harm a fellow coven sister.

"Get out of my way," Roderick snarled as he shoved the other witch.

Hand raised, she muttered an incantation.

"Don't," Roderick said to her as they passed. "I don't want to hurt you, Blessed, but my duty here is clear."

Maeve didn't hear the other witch's response because they were already running down the corridor again. Beatrice. That had been her name. Beatrice.

"She was gathering her magic to use against me," Maeve said, panting as Roderick increased their pace.

"Aye." He slammed the kitchen door open and dragged her behind him, shielding her with his body. "And that isn't the worst of today."

"It's Maeve," someone shrieked. "Get her."

Roderick shifted, his shoulders bunching. He punched. A fist hit flesh. They were moving again.

"Watch yourself." Roderick lifted her over the prone form of a fallen sister.

Roderick. Always the perfect gentleman, gallant to a fault Roderick, who would hack a limb off rather than injure a woman, had punched one of her coven sisters and left her insensible on the floor.

"My duty was clear," he said, as if he despised himself in that moment.

"Indeed." Maeve surprised herself with her lack of sympathy for the fallen witch. "I can only be glad that you consider me to be your duty, and not a hindrance."

He threw her a glance over his shoulder made up of equal parts amusement and bemusement.

Chaos reigned in the bailey. Witches ran this way and that, so quickly she couldn't see who was who.

Through the gate came the villagers, streaming into the bailey with murder in their eyes. A man caught sight of them and shouted.

"Damn." Roderick's grip on her hand tightened. "They got in faster than I thought possible."

"They shouldn't be here at all."

A man grabbed her cloak, almost yanking her off her feet.

Roderick spun, grabbed the man's wrist and twisted.

A sickening crack of bone made Maeve shudder.

The man screamed and dropped to his knees, cradling his wrist to his chest.

"Wards are down, nothing to stop them," Roderick said. "Fiona helped Rhiannon lower them from the inside."

"Why?" She jerked to a stop.

"It doesn't matter now." Roderick dragged her back into motion. "She's not even bothering with a pretense anymore."

But it did matter to her. Why had Fiona betrayed her coven sisters and ushered this mayhem into Baile?

A woman screamed.

Maeve's steps faltered.

A large man, perhaps the village blacksmith, dragged a screaming witch into the bailey by her hair.

"Let's show this bitch how to act as she should." His intent was written clearly on his face.

"You have to help her." Maeve tugged Roderick to a stop. "Even now she's forbidden from using magic to defend herself. You have to help her."

The blacksmith tossed his victim to the ground at his friend's feet.

Men closed on her.

Hester, a young apprentice, hadn't enough magic to defend herself even if Goddess hadn't forbidden its use.

"Help her." Maeve yanked at Roderick's grip on her arm.

"My duty is clear." Roderick shackled both her wrists and dragged her through the sea door to the staircase leading down to the caverns.

Behind them, Hester screamed, and kept on screaming.

Maeve struggled against Roderick. She threw herself this way, and then that. If he wouldn't let go of her, they'd both tumble to their deaths on the rocks below.

With a growl, Roderick upended her over his shoulder and took the remaining stairs at a run.

Inside the caverns, he right sided her so suddenly her head swam, and she almost lost her balance.

Roderick shoved her at someone. "Keep her here."

Maeve swung to fight him, but Roderick was already running up the stairs.

Strong, male hands tugged her back into the cavern. "I'll tie you up if I have to," Thomas said. None of his usual humor showed on his face. "You're safe here, and he can help others."

"Come." Colleen took her hand. "Coimhdeacht always act out of their sworn duty first."

A handful of blessed huddled in the caverns. Most of them, like her, still in their bedclothes. Looking grim and resolved, coimhdeacht were guarding the entrance to the caverns. The witches in the caverns were mostly bonded sisters. She and Roderick now knew who was on their side, but there were far too few.

There had to be others still out there, others like young Hester.

Roderick appeared and pushed a pale and shaken woman inside.

It was Hester. Sobbing, bruised and bleeding from a split lip, she shook convulsively. Other sisters rushed to tend her.

Roderick disappeared up the stairs. Maeve wanted to chase after him and apologize. Again. She should have known he wouldn't leave Hester like that.

Four coimhdeacht stumbled into the caverns. Blood streaking his features, one of them yelled, "There are too many of them and they keep coming. Most of the healthy witches fight with them."

"The passage to the village." Thomas herded witches deeper into the caverns to the secret entrance. "Let's get the sisters to the village green. Our best chance is to separate."

"But Roderick is still out there." Maeve stared down the empty corridor leading to the entrance.

Thomas grabbed her arm. "No, Maeve. You come with us."

"He needs help." Maeve couldn't bear to leave Roderick.

"Maeve." Thomas shook her. "I vowed to him I'd get you to safety. Now go."

He shoved her so hard she stumbled toward the wall.

"The incantation." Colleen glanced about her. Tears had dried on her face, leaving rivulets in the sweat and dust. "I don't know it."

Maeve stepped forward and murmured the incantation. Air without the odor of blood and hatred, air clear of smoke, swept out of the tunnel.

"Come." Colleen kept her arm around Hester. "Our coimhdeacht fight, but the longer we tarry, the more the danger to them."

That's what it took to get a bonded sister to move. They slipped into the tunnel in a line. Fourteen, thirteen full powered witches and Hester the apprentice. And her.

The coimhdeacht formed a protective ring around the passage entrance.

Her heart behind her with Roderick, Maeve followed the others through the tunnel. He was alive, she knew that much through their bond. A jumble of powerful emotions blasted from him; fury, determination, and a growing stoic acceptance. Like Roderick was preparing for eventual failure.

Maeve sent everything she had through the bond, seeking to bolster him and give him her strength to draw from.

Renewed purpose came back to her.

Up ahead, a patch of dark lighter than the gloom surrounding them appeared.

She stumbled through and nearly ran into the back of a witch in front of her.

Their group had stopped and were all staring at something.

A woman with raven colored hair walked toward them across the green. In a silver gown that outlined all her curves, she was breathtaking, and shrouded in blood magic so deep it made Maeve gag.

"Well done." She clapped and chuckled. "You're the witches who survived." She cocked her head, her dark eyes amiable and warm. "Regrettably, I can't allow that to continue."

"Rhiannon," Maeve whispered. She'd never seen her, but she knew down to her marrow.

Rhiannon's gaze fastened on her. "Very clever, my little spirit walker. You have caused me some difficulty recently."

Maeve wasn't sorry, not with Roderick's strength waning. "I'd have made it more if I could."

"Indeed." Rhiannon looked regretful. "But I need to cut that short as well."

"What's this all about?" Colleen's voice shook, but she straightened her shoulders and stepped to the front of the group. "You can't win."

Rhiannon grimaced and giggled. "I'm afraid that I can, and I am. Even now the last of the witches still in Baile are being captured or killed. If they are not for me, then I'll have to send them beyond." She leaned closer and whispered, "You see, your goddess is only as powerful as her witches. When I eliminate you, I render her as weak as a newborn kitten."

"Only one can live." The voices of the first three whispered in Maeve's head. Her breath misted in the suddenly freezing air.

Her coven sisters looked around in amazement.

Vapor streamed from the passage and coalesced into three witches on the green between them and Rhiannon.

"Who are they?" Colleen's eyes rounded as she stared. "Are they..."

"The first." Maeve wondered how they could be amongst the living.

"You." Rhiannon's beautiful features twisted. "You can do nothing here. You're too late. Again."

"Spirit Walker." Tahra looked at her. "Yours is to bear the burden."

"What?" Maeve looked about her at the others.

They were all staring at her.

"Only one can survive," Tahra said.

"So mote it be." Pale but determined, Colleen nodded. She held her hands out to the two witches beside her. "We must form a circle."

"What are you doing?" Maeve stared in horror as her sisters gathered around her. "All of us will survive. We must fight together."

"This is the only way," Tahra said. "We have only strength enough to send one into the fade."

A wave of blood magic rippled through the air. As it hit, witches dropped to their knees, bent over, two even collapsed. Still they formed their circle.

Magic billowed from Rhiannon like a deadly, oily, black cloak.

"She uses the dead witches to draw her power," Tahra said. "We must do the same or the cré-witches are lost forever."

Colleen straightened suddenly and looked at Maeve. "It has to be you."

The other witches wore the same expression Colleen did. Resigned.

"No." Everything in Maeve rejected what she saw.

"The ancients know what must be done and they're drawing on Baile to reach us." Colleen smiled at Maeve. "They've told us what must be done."

"That's impossible." Maeve wanted to be sick. "They only speak to me."

"They give their all to do this," Colleen said. "We accept our fate."

Maeve spun to look at Lavina. "You can't support this. There has to be another way. Thomas fights—"

"Thomas fights no more." Heartbreak etched lines in Lavina's face as she gripped the hands of the witches either side of her. "You're the only one who can walk amongst the dead witches. All their knowledge is your knowledge."

"Our blood will seal this magic. Our lives will give it power." Colleen reached for her birth element.

Maeve couldn't contemplate what they were doing. "We are forbidden blood magic."

"We have no choice." Colleen closed her eyes.

"Come, Maeve." Hester gave her a wan smile. "All of us must do all we can."

"What are you doing?" Rhiannon screamed, but she hit an invisible barrier and bounced back. "You don't dare."

"We don't have much time." Fresh tears streaked Lavina's face. "The first can't hold her for long."

"Our power wanes," Tahra whispered. "Bear the burden you were chosen for. Do it for all the cré-witches to come."

The first spoke as one. "This is the way."

"This is the way." The living witches echoed them.

"There has to be another way." Maeve couldn't move her feet.

Colleen nodded to the other witches. They all nodded back. "It must be done."

"What? What must be done?" The looks on her coven sisters' faces terrified her, even more than the massive tempest of magic snarling and shrieking around Rhiannon.

Somewhere Roderick was still fighting. Their bond was still holding, which meant he was alive. "Roderick will come for us."

"I have come too far to fail now." Rhiannon battered her magic against the wall holding her back. She grabbed a young man and slit his throat, sinking her hands into the blood as it poured from his neck. Her power grew twice the size of the village, blocking out the night sky.

"Now!" Colleen sank to her knees. She pulled a dagger from her belt and cut her wrists.

"No!" Maeve screamed.

Colleen passed the dagger to the witch beside her. One by one, they slit their wrists, knelt and pressed their flowing wounds into the earth.

18

M aeve's limbs were caught in a binding spell.

"Bide, Spirit Walker." Tahra's voice was an insubstantial breeze as she fought to keep Rhiannon at bay. "It is time to take up your burden."

Rhiannon's power built like a thunderstorm, whipping their hair and tugging their clothing.

The ancients held her back, but they were growing more and more insubstantial.

"Mother forgive us," Colleen chanted, and the other witches took up her refrain. "Goddess forgive us."

She was stuck. The breath seeped out of Maeve's lungs. Every passing second, her sisters crept closer to death, and she could do nothing. She opened her mouth and screamed her denial, but no sound escaped her.

Bearing a man across his shoulders, a coimhdeacht stumbled out of the passage. Blood streamed down his face and mingled with sweat and dirt. His chemise was torn in places and stuck to his skin with dried blood. "It is done," he gasped. "Baile is overrun. We're lost."

Roderick. Where was he? But she couldn't speak.

Colleen raised her hands. Blood streamed down her arms, and she swayed. "From the north, I call earth." Green light crackled between her hands. The fetid miasma of blood magic fouled it. "I love you, Sister. Guard our knowledge well."

Colleen sagged.

Maeve's scream stuck in her throat.

Lavina raised her hands. "From the east, I call air." Yellow light swirled about her and then into the green in a dizzying, billowing spiral. The blood magic consumed it hungrily.

A third witch called south. Crumpled forms littered the circle as they gave their lives and their magic into this one, last desperate working.

From the tunnel a tall form burst. He jumped the circled witches and grabbed her hands.

He was here, fierce and strong, and the only steady point in the nightmare.

Wrapping her in his arms, Roderick tucked her into his body to shield her. The calluses on Roderick's battle-hardened hand pressed into her nape.

Muffled by his hold on her, the call to west still reached Maeve. "From the west, I call water."

"Goddess, hear your blessed," the remaining witches chanted, but their voices were soft and pained, fading. "We cast in four for this your spell." The words lost meaning for Maeve.

Lavina's voice rose. "Goddess hold still the march of time. Take into your living death this blessed and her coimhdeacht to protect her."

Already darkness was creeping around the edges of Maeve's vision, pulling at her, tugging at her to come and join it.

"Guard well this sister and her coimhdeacht until it be mote time moves again." Colleen's sweet voice spoke on.

"Wherever you go," Roderick whispered. "I'll be there to protect you. By your side in all."

Magic surged through Maeve like an ice blade, running

through her veins, fusing her muscles, dragging searing blackness with it.

She lost the sound of her sisters' voices, the chill of the night, the shush of the sea and the distant sound of Rhiannon shouting. Only Roderick's steady arms, and the darkness rising, ever rising...

EPILOGUE

CRÉ-WITCH CHRONICLES

resent day

P Alexander watched the small knot of tourists gather around the statue dominating the swathe of velvety grass of the village green.

"They call them The Lovers." The tour guide gestured to the statue behind her. She gave her group a simpering smile. "For obvious reasons."

Cameras and cell phones aimed and took pictures of the statue of a large man, his arms tenderly clasping a woman. You couldn't see the woman's face because it was tucked into his chest. The asinine name had sprung up about two hundred years back and stuck. The only good thing about it was how much it would have gotten up Roderick's arse.

A doe-eyed thirty-something American stared up at the statue. "Who are they?"

Alexander recognized the type. A mail-in-ancestry-kit addict here to trace her roots, and not the one he was looking for. The one he sought rubbed like steel wool against his senses, her magic sweet and tart. He breathed deep. Honey and sage might just become his favorite combination.

"We're not quite sure who they are." The tour guide plastered her candy-floss grin on again. She winked and leaned closer. "Rumor has it he's the original owner of Baile Castle, Sir Roderick."

Rumor got it right in this instance.

Alexander dismissed the Asian couple as not the source. It had been so long since he'd felt that unique pull, it had taken him a few minutes to put a name to it. He'd tracked the trickle of magic to the village green, and finally to the small group surrounding the statue.

There! He zeroed in on the diminutive redhead behind a tall German woman wearing a *Man U* sweatshirt.

No more than five two, she was still a tasty little armful with her shapely curves and big green eyes.

She glanced up and caught him looking.

Alexander smiled at her.

She blushed and went back to listening to the tour guide.

The German woman pointed at the statue. "What happened to Sir Roderick?"

"Another mystery." The tour guide grimaced.

Alexander could have told her exactly what happened to the whoreson.

"Some say it was magic." The tour guide widened her eyes and giggled. "That he just disappeared one night, never to be seen again."

The group gave an obliging chuckle. All except the little honey and sage sweetheart.

Alexander kept his focus on her.

She frowned and chewed on her lip. Then she rubbed her arms and shivered. She felt it all right, the power emanating from the statue.

"Other legends talk of a mass suicide, and another one links his death to the witch hunts of the sixteen-hundreds." The tour guide loved this bit. The village tourist council insisted she drag the groups through the village and try to get them to spend some money in local businesses while they were there. You could take a seat at the Copper Cauldron and pay too much for a tired cheese and ham sandwich or force down that green piss they called Love Potion #9 at the pub, colorfully named The Hag's Head. Other than the statue, however, Greater Littleton was as interesting as day-old bread. The tourists came for the crown in the jewel, Baile Castle.

"Are we going to see the castle soon?" The American thirty-something's burly husband stepped forward. "I came to see the castle."

The rest of the group nodded.

Alexander's prey looked up at the castle perched on the hill above the town and paled. He'd bet she'd seen it before, haunting her dreams, calling to her.

The tour guide checked her watch, lips pursed in irritation. Someone always wanted to cut her tour short. "I'm afraid we'll have to wait another half an hour before we have access to the castle." She gave the American a minatory stare. "The castle is still privately owned, and the owner is most specific about the times they will allow tours."

"Privately owned? Jesus." The American grunted and stared up at the castle. "I wouldn't want to pay the heating bill on that."

Alexander let his gaze stray from his prey to Baile. Gray stone turrets rising against the sky, she was the most intact and beautiful castle in all of England. The only people more surprised to see the little cré-witch than him would be the bitches rattling around in that castle.

～

If you enjoyed this story, and would like to know what happens with Roderick & Maeve. If you would also like a trip to present day, don't miss Born In Water.

AN ANCIENT PROPHECY BINDS THEM.

The women in Bronwyn Beaty's family are cursed; they die young and suddenly. Desperate for answers, Bronwyn's search leads her to a castle in the south of England and straight onto her predestined path.

Created to fulfill the same ancient prophecy as Bronwyn, Alexander walks the knife-edge of being the son of great evil while hiding his deadly secret desire to redeem himself.

Alexander and Bronwyn's connection is immediate and overpowering. Together they must navigate the treacherous waters of evil witch Rhiannon's growing lust for power and Bronwyn's fate to wake the cardinal water point.

Danger escalates, magic grows, and Roderick and Maeve are called upon to guide the vulnerable and near-extinct Baile coven back to Goddess and the rebirth of cré-magic.

Order Born In Water

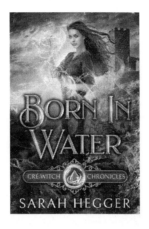

Chapter 1

A beautiful English summer's day greeted Alexander and his morning coffee—as good a day as any to fulfill his fate. In movies days that defined a hero's fate demonstrated a preponderance of stormy weather, at least a dark cloud or two. Perhaps today's sunny outlook was more in the nature of a commentary on his eligibility for heroism.

He walked through the glass doors between his drawing room and the garden and took a deep breath of the flower-scented air. Green swathes of lawn mowed into stripes ended at a rough-hewn fence. Beyond that, stretched acres and acres of pasture he rented to the farmer next door. Birds sang, bees buzzed and cattle lowed, all beneath a gentle sherbet-yellow sun.

Not a day to suggest dark thoughts or even grimmer senses of foreboding, but there you had it. His premonition had ripped him awake at four-thirty, and he'd not gone back to sleep. The details remained confoundedly vague, but he'd seen her clear as day: a curvy redhead with big green eyes. The scent of honey and sage had chased him awake. Unable to go back to sleep, he'd gotten up, worked out in his home gym and tried to escape the dark augury buggering up his morning.

Portents, auguries, evil and darkness brought his thoughts to their inevitable end: Mother.

~

For first dibs on news, deals, and giveaways, and so much more, join the @Home Collective

Or if Facebook is more your thing, join the Sarah Hegger Collective

Anything and everything you need to know on my website http://sarahhegger.com

ABOUT THE AUTHOR

Born British and raised in South Africa, Sarah Hegger suffers from an incurable case of wanderlust. Her match? A hot Canadian engineer, whose marriage proposal she accepted six short weeks after they first met. Together they've made homes in seven different cities across three different continents (and back again once or twice). If only it made her multilingual, but the best she can manage is idiosyncratic English, fluent Afrikaans, conversant Russian, pigeon Portuguese, even worse Zulu and enough French to get herself into trouble. Mimicking her globe trotting adventures, Sarah's career path began as a gainfully employed actress, drifted into public relations, settled a moment in advertising, and eventually took root in the fertile soil of her first love, writing. She also moonlights as a wife and mother. She currently lives in Ottawa, Canada, filling her empty nest with fur babies. Part footloose buccaneer, part quixotic observer of life, Sarah's restless heart is most content when reading or writing books.

[facebook icon]

PRAISE FOR SARAH HEGGER

Drove All Night
"The classic romance plot is elevated to a modern-day, wholly accessible real-life fairy tale with an excellent mix of romantic elements and spicy sensuality."
Booklife Prize, Critic's Report

Positively Pippa
"This is the type of romance that makes readers fall in love not just with characters, but with authors as well."
Kirkus Review (Starred Review)

"What begins as a simple second-chance romance quickly transforms into a beautiful, frank examination of love, family dynamics, and following one's dreams. Hegger's unflinching, candid portrayal of interpersonal and generational communication elevates the story to the sublime. Shunning clichés and contrived circumstances, she uses realistic, relatable situations to create a world that readers will want to visit time and again."
Publisher's Weekly, Starred Review

Hegger's utterly delightful first Ghost Falls contemporary is what other romance novels want to grow up to be." – Publisher's Weekly, Best Books of 2017

"The very talented Hegger kicks off an enjoyable new series set in the small Utah town of Ghost Falls. This charming and fun-filled book has everything from passion and humor to betrayal and revenge." – Jill M Smith, RT Books Reviews 2017 – Contemporary Love and Laughter Nominee

Becoming Bella
"Hegger excels at depicting familial relationships and friendships of all kinds, including purely platonic friendships between women and men. Tears, laughter, and a dollop of suspense make a memorable story that readers will want to revisit time and again."
Publisher's Weekly, Starred Review

"...you have a terrific new romance that Hegger fans are going to love. Don't miss out!"
Jill M. Smith – RT Book Reviews

Blatantly Blythe
"Ms. Hegger has delivered another captivating read for this series in this book that was packed with emotion..." Bec, Bookmagic Review, Harlequin Junkie, HJ Recommends.

Nobody's Fool
"Hegger offers a breath of fresh air in the romance genre." – Terri Dukes, RT Book Reviews

Nobody's Princess
"Hegger continues to live up to her rapidly growing reputation

for breathing fresh air into the romance genre." – Terri Dukes, RT Book Reviews

"I have read the entire Willow Park Series. I have loved each of the books ... Nobody's Princess is my favorite of all time." Harlequin Junkie, Top Pick

ALSO BY SARAH HEGGER

Printed in Great Britain
by Amazon